Forging Destiny

STAND-ALONE NOVEL

A Western Historical Adventure Book

by

Zachary McCrae

Disclaimer & Copyright

This is a work of fiction. Names, characters, places and incidents either are products of the author's imagination or are used fictitiously. Any resemblance to actual events or locales or persons, living or dead, is entirely coincidental.

Table of Contents

Letter from Zachary McCrae

I'm a man who loves plain things; a cup of strong coffee in the morning, a good book at noon and his wife's embrace at night. I want to write stories that take you from the hand and show you what it meant to be someone who tried to make ends meet and find their own way in 19-century United States. I've been this someone for a long time in my life, always looking for my next gig after my parents' sudden death, always finding new friends but somehow not being able to stick with 'em. It's easy to find quantity in your life but what about quality?

At the age of 50, and after my baby boy, Jeb, and my sweet daughter, Janette, went away to study East, with my sweet wife, Mrs. Maryanne Mc Crae, we moved back to my home town and my dad's ranch close to the Rockies. After a series of health issues that have brought me even closer to our Lord, I've officially started writing those stories I always loved to read. I'm tending my land and animals now with the help of Maryanne, and I'm grateful for each day I get to walk on this world we call earth. As the saying goes, "Nature gave us all something to fall back on, and sooner or later we all land flat on it," so I want to take care of it just the way it has taken care of my dad and mom, and my cousins.

My adventure stories are my legacy to my children and to all of the readers that will honor me by following my work. God bless you and your families and our land! Thank you.

Stay safe but adventurous,

Zachary McCrae

Prologue

Morgan Ranch

New York

April 12, 1861

Boom!

A rumble of thunder rolled through the valley, shaking the earth with the portent of a coming storm. Ominous black clouds massed in the east, rolling and surging into dark-tipped waves. The storm's peculiar greenish tint covered the fields and lit up the pale pink blooms of the budding apple trees to a sickly yellow.

Crack!

As Luke Morgan glanced up from his fiery forge, a ragged fork of lightning split the sky. The scene through his window promised nature's fury before long.

"Luke! Luke!" his wife, Betty shouted from the veranda of their home. Her voice rose in a frightened moan as she twisted a damp apron. "Luke!"

He dropped the horseshoe he'd been hammering into a bucket of cool water. Hurrying to the door of his workshop, Luke called out, "What's wrong?"

"Find Hannah! She's run off again. The storm..."

The wind chose that second to whip into a fury, shaking the trees and slamming the door to Luke's workshop. *I'm coming,* it seemed to announce. *Run, get indoors, protect those you love.*

"I'll bring her in," he promised. A lean, well-groomed man, Luke kept his wheat-colored beard trimmed, his light hair tucked neatly behind each ear. His blue eyes were keen and observant. Steady hands and an unruffled temperament kept him on an even keel with life. Known throughout his community as a trustworthy and respected gunsmith, Luke worked hard to live a godly, peaceful life. "Billy!" Luke called for his seven-year-old son. Early that morning, when Luke headed to his smithy, Billy had tagged along like a persistent shadow. Until Betty's call, Luke had thought Hannah, holding a squirming puppy, had been nearby too. "Where's your sister?"

Billy ran up, having a hard time staying upright with the fierce pushing of the wind. Unlike his mother, who despised storms, Billy let the wind tug him playfully backward. His wind-blown blond hair swished over his twinkling blue eyes. "In the barn?"

"Let's find her before the storm."

One of their prized mares had given birth to a colt a few days before. Hannah couldn't get her fill of staring at the foal.

On the way to the barn, Luke stopped a second to glance down the long, pea gravel drive toward the house—a white clapboard two stories high with a grand veranda across the front. His father had built the beginnings of a small log cabin and the house had expanded as the family's prosperity grew. A sturdy house, capable of weathering any storm nature cared to send. But not the ones human hate could devise.

What if a war comes here?

The papers were full these days of ominous warnings, more threatening than the rolling clouds massing in the sky. *No time for that now.* Luke's long legs increased their stride as he hurried toward the barn.

As Billy predicted, they found Hannah in the barn, peering through the slats of the mare's stall. Hannah's blue eyes gazed through a mop of blond curls. One small fist clenched the slat of the stall. In the other, she held out an oatmeal cookie toward the foal.

"Hannah, horses can't eat cookies. You silly girl."

"It's so big for a baby, Poppa," Hannah said as Luke swooped the four-year-old up into his arms. Leaning in he kissed her baby cheeks, delighting in her chuckle, the sturdy little body. "How come?"

"Even though a colt's a baby, it's big. Big enough to grow into a horse like Daisy. Come along. A storm's coming." Luke dusted off the front of her white pinafore covered with prickly strands of hay. "What'd you do, roll around on the barn floor?"

From the house, the loud clanging of the dinner bell rang through the rising wind. Calling them to lunch.

"Hurry, let's run before the rain!" He grabbed up Hannah and clutched Billy's sweaty hand.

I'm truly blessed with everything a man could desire. A fine wife, children, a prosperous home and business, good friends, and health. What more could a man need?

Luke took none of his blessings for granted. Ever since President Lincoln's election the previous November, the South had had more reasons to grumble. This morning's newspapers had left Luke with growing concerns. He shook off his unreasonable fears and hurried toward the house with a single glance backward at the clouds scurrying toward the house.

Looks like a gully-washer.

Inside, Betty hurried around, lighting the oil lamps to shake off the gloom in the dining room. Outside the wind howled and doors slammed from hidden drafts. “Oh, dear!” Betty exclaimed each time, terrified of nature’s fury. “I dislike storms!”

Another clap of thunder shook the house, followed by a blinding flash of lighting. Hannah squealed, clapped her hands. “God just lit a big big candle,” she sang.

“It’s just a little wind and rain,” Luke teased, helping to settle Billy and Hannah at their places around the table. Freshly washed, the children’s faces shone. Secure in their safety, they talked and laughed without a care in the world.

Silverware gleamed and glasses sparkled on the neatly set table. Mrs. O’Shay would have it no other way. The stout, red-cheeked cook bustled in with a tureen of pea soup and placed it beside Betty. A frown puckered her face.

“Here you go, ma’am. It’s fixin’ to pour any second now. Sure an’ I hope the creek doesna flood.”

Window panes rattled and Betty jumped. Lunch proceeded as outside the sky grew darker and a small pattering of raindrops plucked at the windows.

They were finished with the soup and had begun on a platter of beef steaks when the door from the kitchen slammed against the wall. A shelf of Betty’s China knick knacks rattled and even Luke jumped as a dripping man ran into the room.

“Luke, Ma’am.” Mr. O’Shay pulled off his gray hat as he hurried into the elegant dining room. Wearing rumpled farm clothes and muddy boots, he shifted uneasily on the dark, floral carpet. An anxious furrow creased his leathery forehead. Mr. O’Shay was married to the cook and helped farm Luke’s substantial acreage. He had never, to Luke’s remembrance, burst into a room in such a way. Not even the day all the cows had escaped the pasture fence. "Excuse me botherin' but it's here!"

Behind him, Mrs. O'Shay scurried in, cheeks pale, hands clasped in prayer.

A shudder ran along Luke's spine, a sensation his mother used to call "someone walking over my grave."

"What happened?" Betty questioned. "What's here? The storm?"

"Them folks in the south. They took guns an' fired at a place called Fort Sumter. It's here! They're sayin' down at the telegraph office."

Luke dropped his fork. Around him the children kept eating, unaware of the importance of the news. Suddenly, the heavy pelting of rain thundered against the roof, unleashing an epic fury as if the clouds had burst.

"I don't understand," Betty spoke up. "What does it mean?"

"War."

Chapter One

Morgan Ranch

New York Valley

One Year Later

"I don't want you to go. They can't ask it of me or you."

Lying beside him in bed, Betty couldn't stop weeping.

"Bets," Luke pulled her close and tried to assure her. "I won't be on a battlefield. I'll be safe as a baby in a cradle. Just stuck away in a workroom somewhere making guns. The only difference will be you can't run out to the smithy and talk with me. Or bring me some of Mrs. O'Shay's good coffee."

"Why?" Betty lamented. "Why did that telegram have to come today?"

Needed at once. Weapon repairs at front. War progressing.

"Oh, Luke," Betty moaned, "I'd hoped you wouldn't be drawn into this. Things were going so well here."

"I know."

It had been a long year, yet peaceful, since the war began. Luke had stayed home, doing repairs for the Army under the direction of General Grant. Until the telegram came, his family had been untouched by war. Betty had not taken the idea of his leaving gracefully.

He drew her into his arms, tucking her face against his chest. Betty's head had always fit in the niche between his heart and his chin. "If they say I'm safe, they won't have me on the battlefield. I'll probably be stuck in a barn somewhere. Doing the same thing I'm doing here."

"But we won't see you. The children...the servants..."

"You'll have lots of help and I know you'll be safe here. The war hasn't even come close to us. People in other states are suffering so much more than we are."

Betty pressed her face against his bare chest.

He felt silent weeping as her body shook. "How can they ask this of you?"

"The US Department or Ordnance can and will call me to serve my country," Luke told her gently, stroking her back. Although he tried to speak in a calm voice, he quaked inside, dreading what might lie ahead. "There's a colonel, Hiram Berdan. He's getting together a regiment of sharpshooters. I'm told he needs good weapons, not those old falling-apart pieces most of the men bring with them. I can make a difference by supplying them with well-made rifles. Maybe save some of their lives by giving them usable firearms."

To kill other men. It was not a thought Luke wanted to entertain for long.

"I don't want you to go," she wept again. Warm tears wet his chest as tears filled his own eyes.

"I know," he whispered, "I know. Don't say anything to anyone else yet. We'll tell the children and the servants tomorrow. It will be all right. Before you know it, I'll be coming home."

Soon. Soon I'll be back to them. This war can't last much longer.

***

West Virginia

Sunday, April 9, 1865

Luke picked up his pen, glancing with anticipation at the empty paper on his desk. Filling those pages with news for Betty, sharing stories of camp, helped connect him to the home he missed so much. *I've been gone so long.* Each Sunday, he looked forward to the brief, quiet time when he could dip his pen in ink and write to his loved ones. His fond smile changed to a puzzled frown as a new sound began to drown out the usual quiet Sunday noises. Whoops and cheers, growing closer every moment.

"Luke!"

Greg Bennet, a friend from the Quartermaster Department, rushed into the tent. "It's over! Lee surrendered to Grant at Appomattox! A messenger just brought the news. The Union won! We won!"

Luke jumped up and the rickety table crashed to the floor, spilling ink and paper. Betty's letter sailed into every corner of the tent. He crushed the just-written reply in his hand. "Over?"

The news was so unexpected and startling, Luke could only stand and stare. Unbelieving.

The jubilant expression on Greg's leathery, care-worn face finally convinced him it wasn't a joke. "It's over! The war is over!" The older man's joyous blue eyes gleamed with a sparkle that left no doubt.

Outside the tent the other men in the unit whooped and hollered. Someone shot off a volley of bullets into the air. It was a day of celebration. A day to rejoice! After four long, grueling years, the North had won. Men laughed, cried, and banged on every pot and pan cook had in the mess tent. The noise was one loud hurrah of rejoicing. Jubilation!

"I won't have to mail this now. I'll tell Betty the news in person." Luke shouted over the din, ripping the letter in two. "I can tell her in person." A lightness came over him; almost as if he'd dropped the weight of the war he'd carried on his shoulders. His heart felt as if it might burst with joy.

I'm going home!

Chapter Two

West Virginia

With his discharge papers in hand, Luke wasn't willing to wait one moment longer than necessary to get home. "Where will you go?" he asked Greg as he packed his blue trousers away in the trunk. "Back home? To New Jersey?"

Greg opened the truck at the end of his bunk. Gathered a stack of linen shirts from a rickety dresser. "I'm headed to Council Bluff, Iowa."

"Why there?"

"Going to work on the UPR project. I've already got a job. Locomotive engineer."

"What's that? The UPR?" Luke asked. The initials reminded him of something he'd read, but he couldn't place it.

"The Union Pacific Railroad project. President Lincoln signed it into law as the Pacific Railroad Act in '82. The idea is to span the country from east to west with a railroad track. To unite us from sea to sea. It's going to be the first transcontinental railroad ever built."

"Sounds like a mighty ambitious project. Seems like I've read about it."

"It is," Greg agreed. "Good pay too. I figure to stick with it a few years, then get myself a grub stake somewhere out west. Why don't you come with me? I can put in a word and find you a job."

"Can't. Got the wife and family waiting back home. I've got a gunsmith business and a prosperous ranch. Why would I want to go to Iowa?"

I can't wait to get home!

"Take the family with you," Greg suggested. "Plenty of opportunities out west."

Luke shook his head, not even tempted by the offer. There was only one place he wanted to travel to—home.

***

Morgan Ranch

New York

May 1865

Despite the early start the next morning, and the locomotive's top speed of twenty miles per hour, time chugged by on snail steps. Luke had never been so impatient to get home. At a depot close to his small town outside New York City, he couldn't wait a second longer. The town slept in the gray light of dawn. A month after President Lincoln's assassination, most of the buildings were still draped in black bunting and mourning wreaths. The capture of the murderer had done little to lift spirits.

Such a tragedy. Even with home before him, Luke felt almost as if those black skeins wrapped around his own spirit.

Departing the train, he rented a horse at the Livery, waking a young boy he didn't remember. The lanky, long-limbed boy yawned and scratched the front of a worn gray Union suit through the whole transaction.

I wonder what happened to Mr. Samuels?

Luke didn't spare the time to ask about the man he remembered as the Livery owner before the war. A lot had changed in the years he'd been away.

"Giddup." Luke urged the unfamiliar gelding to gallop the familiar route home. The rutted dirt road had never seemed so long although he knew it was only a short hour's ride from the city. A fine mist wafted up from the chilly ground, swathing the trees and brush in eerie gray shadows. He knew it would warm up later, but for now Luke shuddered in a blue woolen jacket and dark trousers.

As Luke neared the wrought iron gate, stark black in the misty dawn, the horse shied. Snorted. Luke stopped and smiled, resting a hand on the cool metal of Betty's gate. He remembered crafting the fine ironwork gate for Betty that long-ago week after Fort Sumter had been fired upon. Somehow crafting a gate full of "whatnots" and "furbelows", as he'd teased Betty, seemed another lifetime ago. In a world without fear or trouble.

Life will be good again. It must.

Through the swirls of fog, Luke caught sight of the sprawling house at the end of the pea gravel drive. Nothing seemed amiss but the dunderhead horse tossed his mane and refused to budge another inch.

That's what I get for renting a mount. I'll be glad to get into my barn and saddle up Shadow. I wonder if he'll remember me.

"Whoa, boy, whoa." Luke dismounted and wrapped the horse's reins loosely around one of the pointed spikes of Betty's fancy gate. Still solid. Still standing. His lips curved in a smile as he remembered Betty and the children watching as he crafted her elegant gate. It creaked as he swung one side open to walk eagerly up the drive.

That should have been oiled. Titus should have...

Luke's boots kicked up gravel as he hurried up the drive, aware of something off kilter. Wrong. A sudden spasm of fear clenched his heart as he noticed the front windows were shattered. Had the horse sensed something wrong too? A tattered blue drape fluttered through the parlor window. Betty would never have allowed...

"Betty?" He shouted. "Titus!"

No one answered.

Chapter Three

"Don't move!"

Somewhere behind Luke came the ominous sound of a gun being cocked.

"You move an' inch and I'll blow your head off! Who are you? You got no business here."

Kneeling on the cold ground, staring at those crude wooden markers, Luke had no feelings about having his head blown off. Maybe it would be for the better. His whole body felt numb, his mind in turmoil.

It's not true. How can it be true?

"Who are you?" the man hollered again and nudged Luke's shoulder with the barrel of a rifle. "Who...Luke? Is that you?"

Luke turned bleary eyes to face his attacker. The anger drained from the man's weathered face, and he lowered the rifle. "Luke, son, I didn't expect to find you here."

"How did you..."

"I was ridin' past this morning on my way to town and spotted a strange horse hitched to your gate. I figured those marauders had showed back up here."

"What..." Luke stared again at the crude markers, the names burnt into the wood, Betty, Billy, Hannah. "How?"

"I'm right sorry, Luke," Mr. Montgomery, his nearest neighbor, offered his condolences as they stood beside the new graves. "I was a-gonna try to find you and give you the news, but the telegraph we sent come back. Said you had left already."

"What happened? Do you know?"

The man stood with his shoulders stooped as if weary of life. He pointed the rifle toward the ground and sighed. "Well, we'd heard tell there were some Confederates, of all things, setting fires in the city. Trying to raise up the rebellion again, I expect. We didn't think nothing of it. Wasn't until that day I saw the smoke and ran over here..."

A knot formed in Luke's throat. He wanted to know, and he didn't. "Do you know how they died?"

"They died right quick," Mr. Montgomery said as if that offered any comfort. "By the time I saw the smoke and got here, they were all dead. It grieves me to say, but it looked like them low-down cusses raided your workroom and stole the weapons from there."

Killed by gunfire! Guns from my own stockpile!

It was a cruel twist of fate that wrenched Luke's heart into a tight knot. All the love he'd had for his family shriveled like a dried-up apple. He would never love again. Anyone. Or anything.

Why did God allow such a thing to happen? I was helping to preserve the union and my family was slaughtered by marauders. Using my weapons. He wished he could go back in time and never create the guns that had killed his family. But if not the guns, then maybe something worse.

"Me an' the sheriff found the O'Shay's, Titus, Jeff, Rosie, and Abby all the servants shot too. Looked like Titus had tried to save Billy and Hannah."

Poor Titus. He had done what he said—given his life to try to protect my family. Luke remembered that day long ago when he'd left. Titus's reassurances that he'd protect the family.

“What about the other servants? The freed Blacks who worked on shares?”

“Can’t rightly say. We never found no sign of them. I don’t think they run off. They thought too much of you, Luke. If I had to guess, I’d say they were taken prisoner.”

Luke stood—confused and uncertain, not sure his legs would hold him up. How could such a thing happen? Yes, the north had won the war, but not all slaves were free. Not all men agreed to lay down their arms. And not all pillagers were Confederate or Union soldiers. Some simply took advantage of the chaos to loot and destroy. He would never truly know who had ravaged his home and family. Evil forged its own road.

Sadly, my family stood in their path.

“What do you plan to do now? If you want help rebuilding, I can get some of the neighbors to…”

“No, I don’t know. I’m not sure what my plans are.”

“Come on to the house, son.” Mr. Montgomery took his arm as if he were a child. “We'll brew up some coffee and get some food into you. You don’t want to sit out here in the cold and damp.”

Mr. Montgomery had taken him home, but by nightfall Luke had wandered back to his home. What was left of it. He’d revisited the graves, determined one day to give them the fine monuments they deserved.

Luke knew one thing for certain. He would never spend another night in the house where he’d once known such joy. As he’d wandered through the splinters and ash of what had been a happy home, weeping and mourning, Luke had come to a decision. It was time to close a door to the life he’d known and move. There was nothing left for him here.

Greg Bennett had offered him a job working for the Union Pacific Railroad. If the offer still stood, Luke would accept the job. If nothing else, it would put some distance between himself and a heartache too heavy to bear.

After thanking Mr. Montgomery for all he'd done, Luke headed to the small town and to a telegraph office. Before the next morning, he would send word to Greg in Iowa.

Chapter Four

Council Bluffs, Iowa

June 1865

Three Weeks Later

Luke stepped from the train depot into a whirlwind of people and commotion. The noise thundered at his ears until he wanted to tug down the navy-blue slouch hat to cover them. A dozen sounds competed—the rap of hammers, the *clink ching* of chisels hitting rock, the thunder of horse-drawn wagons driving over cobblestones and so many voices in such a multitude of languages it was hard to distinguish a single word in the gibberish. A long, wild scream from the train's whistle ripped through the smoke-filled sky.

"Luke! Luke Morgan!"

A welcome voice called from out of the confusion. Luke turned expectantly toward the summons, relieved to see Greg's familiar, shaggy bearded face. As Luke gripped his satchel, Greg hurried through a milling crowd of people until he could reach out and shake Luke's hand in a firm grip. "I'm glad you made it."

"This is..." Luke couldn't think of words to describe the scene. Even trying to focus on one person, one building caused his head to ache, his eyes to blur.

Greg shook his head and chuckled. "It takes some getting used to for sure. Let's go this way. I booked you a room at the hotel. It's only for a few nights. We'll be moving out to the site in a day or so."

They walked along the teeming streets, edging past men shoving push carts filled with a variety of wares—cabbages, rags, pickaxes, and a dozen other items. Women blocked the way, gossiping and staring, calico dresses worn and wrinkled. Many gaped in frank curiosity at Luke's citified gray suit and neatly combed beard. Dozens of children darted here and there. Luke heard accents he couldn't even fathom and languages foreign to his ears. One dark-haired man passed by wearing a pair of silken trousers in deep red, a long black braid down his back. He nodded and bowed as he passed, hands tucked into the wide flowing sleeves of a dark red tunic.

"Greg," Luke nodded as the man passed. "I've never seen anyone dressed like that."

"Chinaman," Greg supplied. "You'll see a lot of them working on the railroad here. They're steady workers, hard workers. Not that everyone appreciates that fact. We don't have as many working on the UP as the Central Pacific does, but we've managed to snag a few."

Luke remembered learning about China as a schoolboy.

I sure never expected to meet a real Chinaman from half a world away.

"I was real sorry to hear about your family." Greg made his condolences as they walked along. "That had to be hard. Did you find out what happened?"

Even though he didn't like to discuss the painful event, Luke figured he owed Greg an explanation. After all, after he'd settled his affairs in New York, he'd been only too glad to accept Greg's offer of a job. To put as much distance between himself and the memories as possible. "Marauders. Confederates, maybe. Or even just scavengers. There were reports of Confederates setting fires in New York City and roaming out into the countryside. One of my neighbors saw the smoke and hurried over. It was too late."

Luke's throat closed hard over unshed tears. *I should have been there. I should have been home to protect my family.* Even so many weeks later, he couldn't stop the guilt that consumed almost every waking hour. All the "what ifs" he'd tormented himself with.

"I'm sorry."

This time Luke nodded, kept his eyes forward. He'd done his mourning in New York. Mostly. *My cherished life is over.*

Time to move ahead. *Somehow.*

As if he could see Luke didn't want to speak about the tragedy, Greg deftly changed the subject. "Let's go meet a few of the people we'll be working with," he said instead, leading Luke toward a cluster of men near a railroad section in progress.

Luke looked with interest at the wooden ties—hewn from hardwood and placed in a pattern along the length of the road. The scent of creosote filled the air. Soon, he knew, workers would begin to place the iron rails across the top and secure them with spikes as they laid another length of track.

I'll probably be making a good many of those spikes. Billy would be proud to know I'm helping build a railroad.

A small group of Chinese men stood around, holding chisels and picks. Another held a sledgehammer and jabbered in the unknown tongue. A lean, expensively dressed man in a dusty blue suit towered over the shorter men. Red faced; he punctuated angry commands with an expensive cigar between two fingers.

"You're worthless, the lot of you!" he bellowed as Luke and Greg walked up. "I don't know why we have to be saddled with your kind. Get back to work! Now. This section of track needs to be down before the end of the week. Every second we lose costs money!"

The workers stared with unreadable looks, slanted, dark eyes intent and solemn.

"That's Trevor Peterson, he's one of the UP officers." Greg whispered as he came up behind the man. "Trevor, this is the fellow I told you about, Luke Morgan. Luke, this is Trevor Peterson. He's the big boss around here."

The man placed the cigar between his lips and reached out to shake Luke's hand. Trevor's hand felt moist and soft, not like a firm manly handshake. Luke couldn't hide his sudden distaste. I *don't like this guy. He's never done a day's work with his hands.* Luke knew his own hands were calloused and cracked. Although it felt snobbish, Luke couldn't help but judge other men by how hard they worked with their hands. It had been something ingrained in him by his father.

"Never trust a man who doesn't have work roughed hands, son. A man who doesn't toil and sweat, has no integrity."

"Pleased to meet you, Luke. Greg will get you all set up. We'll figure out some of your duties tomorrow. I hear you're a good gunsmith and can do some blacksmithing in a pinch. We've got use for both tasks here. I need someone to help with metal fabrication and Greg here tells me you're an expert. We also need someone to keep our weapons in order." He turned to Greg with a grimace. "Some of the workers out at the western grade had trouble with the Indians again. I had to send a few men out to guard the men dynamiting a rocky hill."

Greg pressed his lips together but didn't reply.

"However I can be of help," Luke said, still not sure what his duties would be or where he'd be working. As Greg had told him, they were all just learning as the project moved ahead.

"Sure, sure," Trevor dismissed Luke. With a look of distaste for the Chinese workers, he shook his head and turned away. He stopped to issue an instruction to Greg. "I need to see you tomorrow." To Luke, it sounded like a threat.

Greg didn't look pleased but agreed.

Wonder what that's all about?

One of the Chinese men stared after Trevor with those inscrutable eyes. Luke gave him a shaky smile, but was met with that silent, measuring stare. *It must be hard for them here. Not speaking the language.*

Luke made a vow to try to learn some of their words so he could communicate.

"I've got to get back to work," Greg said a while later, after helping Luke get settled at the red brick hotel. "I'll come by in the morning and we'll get you started."

"Greg," Luke didn't want to talk about his family again, but he wanted to express his gratitude somehow. "Thank you for..."

He and Greg had been close friends during the war. They'd spent years together and become as close as brothers. A slow smile crinkled behind Greg's mangy brown beard; his blue eyes twinkled. "Wait until you've been on the job a few weeks before you thank me. This might be the worst decision you've ever made. The UP and Trevor Peterson can be worse taskmasters than the Union army."

After a quick wash up in his hotel room, Luke went to find a restaurant for a meal. He entered a clean, homey-looking place with red checked curtains. An appetizing scent of roast beef and yeasty bread were good indications he could fill his stomach. Several tables were filled with men—some cleaner than others. Railroad workers were obvious in dirty shirts with odorous wet patches under their arms. Their sunburnt faces were creased with unwashed dirt deep in the crevices. Filthy hands held silverware in tight fists as they shoveled in food from the China plates.

Luke nodded at several curious stares in his direction. A cheerful, chattering waitress in a neat black dress led him to a table. At one table Luke noticed a man, woman and three small children with clean, shiny faces enjoying a meal.

A pain pierced Luke's heart as he looked at the family. *I wonder if they know how blessed they are.* He thought of Betty, Hannah, and Billy with longing. Billy tagging along, forever chattering questions. Little Hannah, carrying cats or chickens bigger than her small, chubby arms could hold. His sweet Betty, the only woman he'd ever love.

He glanced over again at the table with the family, then forced himself to turn away. To harden his heart.

Never again.

Chapter Five

Labor Camp

Council Bluffs, Iowa

The next few days were a confusing jumble of familiar work, new tasks, and unknown people. Greg showed him to a small shack near the main rail line. "For now, you'll just help when some of the cross ties come and are warped. We need a blacksmith to straighten them out." Greg showed Luke the equipment in the makeshift shed. "I'm going to send Harry along and he can take you further out. We're working on a section where we have scrapers and plows. Sometimes those scrapers hit rock and bend. You'll be needed to repair those so we can keep moving ahead."

Luke knew from Greg's explanation that the scrapers were wide, deep shovels with two short handles. A half hoop of steel curved from one side of the hoop to the other. The horse teams were hitched to the hoop of steel. The scrapers joined the plows in carving out the prairie sod for the laying of the railroad ties.

"Even one scraper out of commission loses time," Greg told him. "And time wasting is one of Trevor's worst enemies."

"Any job I can do," Luke agreed. Staying busy would keep the thoughts about his family out of his mind.

"Well, you'll be a jack of all trades out here," Greg told him. "We've got horses and mules who will need regular shoeing. There will be parts you'll have to fabricate for the trains. Not that you'll be making one from the wheels up, but there will be parts that come loose, other improvements we'll make out here. There'll be tools to sharpen, just about everything you can imagine."

Luke had no doubts about his ability to find a solution to any blacksmithing job Greg could send his way.

Trevor made one short visit to Luke's shed to give him some "rules" about the job. Although later all Luke could remember was that Trevor was boss and wanted everyone to know it. His word was law. He also disliked any other nationality but white men and wasn't afraid to show it. Trevor spiced his speech with filthy slurs against the Chinese, Irish and free Blacks who worked for him.

Remembering Titus and Jeff, Luke's dislike of the man grew.

All men are equal in God's eyes. Trevor has no right to call anyone names.

Those first few days, Luke did little more than sort and organize blacksmithing tools into wooden boxes. Greg had told him a wagon would help him move to the western site any day. Luke wanted to be ready. A couple of men came by to have small adjustments made to rifles and one old Army Colt. Luke knew it was easy work, almost mindless work.

I'd almost be glad of harder work. To keep from remembering.

The third day in camp, Luke made friends with a man named Harry Miles. "I'm working in construction at the camp," Harry said when he introduced himself and shook Luke's hand with a firm leathery grip. "Harry Miles is the name."

A stout, well-fed man with a short bristle of brown hair and merry hazel eyes, he welcomed Luke to the community. Harry oversaw the construction of anything wooden relating to the

UPR. "If it's wooden," he proudly told Luke, "Me and me crew can either build it or repair it."

"Glad to meet you, Harry."

"Got a wife and baby here with me." Harry kept up his cheerful banter. "We'd be pleased to have you to supper one night."

Luke wasn't sure he cared to visit with a happy family just yet. But the invitation pleased him. Other than Greg, Harry was the first friendly person he'd spoken to. Other than the cheerful, apple-cheeked waitress at the Stanley House where he ate meals, Luke didn't speak to many. It was too hard to answer their questions about his life. "Thank you kindly. I'll keep that in mind."

"You got a family, Mr. Morgan?" Harry asked the dreaded question.

For just a second Luke hesitated—unwilling to share his past just yet. "Not anymore."

As if aware the reminder might be inappropriate, Harry said no more on the subject. He quickly changed the conversation to news about building the UP. Luke had no doubt how proud Harry was to be doing the work of spanning the country with the railroad. As Luke found out over the next few days, Harry could be depended upon to offer helpful advice or suggestions. He seemed to know everything about everyone and didn't mind sharing. After that one probing question, Harry didn't ask Luke anything else about his family.

"Mr. Peterson says you're the man to see," Harry said and showed Luke to a cart filled with tools, dull saws and chisels. "Got to have all these sharpened before Friday."

"I'll get right on it," Luke promised, wiping the sweat from his brow. Repairing tools was simple but time-consuming work.

I'm glad to keep busy.

Keeping busy meant less time to think. With tools, axles, wagon wheels, and horses and mules to be shod, Luke found enough variety of work that he had to ask Mr. Peterson for apprentices. It took hours to forge and repair the metal components of the scrapers. To put new rims on wheels and replace broken axles. Luke was glad for the back-breaking work that kept him busy during the day and too weary to think most nights.

Over the next several days, Luke and Harry moved to set up a makeshift forge near the current section of track building. As part of the construction crew, Harry and his men took one day to build an open-air shed to house Luke's forge and a worktable for jobs. The shed and tools had to be ready to move at a moment's notice as the railroad lines cut deeper across the swells of prairie grass.

"You'll move along with the track building," Harry explained, "so you'll be right there where we need your skills."

Luke came to know Harry well. He met Harry's wife, Julie, and their three-month-old baby, Bonnie. Julie often brought Harry's lunch in a tin pail and after a few days, she took to bringing extra for Luke.

"You don't need to do that," he tried to dissuade her one afternoon. His stomach rumbled at the appetizing scent of fresh dough and beef in something Julie called a "pastie."

She wiped off a slab plank table and spread a cheerful gingham napkin over the top. Almost like something Betty would have done—create civilization in a wild, untamed place.

"I know I don't need to," Julie said, "but this food is better than you'll get at the Stanley House. Or eat at the mess tent. Besides," she waved her hand around at the dust, dirt and activity surrounding the open-air shed, "you'd have to ride all the way back into town to buy lunch. Bonnie and I brought it out here."

It was true. Luke had wondered about eating meals so far from town. The Labor Camp had a mess tent. Greg had told him he could eat there as most of the other laborers did. But, somehow, Luke disliked the idea of crowding into a tent and facing dozens of questions. Other than Greg and Harry, he tried to keep his distance from the other construction workers so far.

People are too curious.

While Harry held baby Bonnie, jiggling her up and down to make her smile, Julie set out the food.

"You best be agreein'," Harry said with a proud grin at his wife, "me Julie won't take no for an answer."

"Well..."

"Eat." Julie commanded, with a fist to the hip of her dark blue calico. "I want to catch a ride back to town with someone."

Luke had no choice but to obey. As he shared the delicious food, he thought of Betty with a pang.

I miss her every day.

One lunchtime, Luke got his first inkling all was not right with Trevor. That not all the workers on the UP project were happy with him or the way he handled his responsibilities.

"Luke?" Trevor hurried up, shoving a wide-brimmed gray hat back on his head. He pulled a dusty handkerchief from his pocket and swabbed at the dirt and sweat on his forehead. Although he swiped the linen over his sunburned face, it did little to clean. "Blast this filthy country! I need..."

It was lunchtime and today Harry had carried the tin pail of lunch from Julie. Harry had just opened the pail and passed Luke a hunk of bread wrapped in a cloth napkin.

"What are you doing here, Harry?" Trevor interrupted his summons of Luke, a frown made furrows across his face.

"Havin' me lunch, Mr. Peterson. The UP's not agin' that are they?"

Trevor shook his head. "Don't be a fool. Don't dawdle too long. I need some timber built to shore up a ditch about ten feet ahead. The wood is cut to specs and piled up for you. You'll have to get those Chinamen to carry it out. I can't spare a wagon."

As if he planned to enjoy his lunch despite the orders, Harry pulled out two napkin-wrapped chunks of ham and passed one to Luke.

"Morgan!" Trevor snapped. "There are two wagons out of commission this afternoon. Get them fixed and back out there today. We're losing time and time is money."

Luke bit back an angry reply. *I'm working as fast as I can.* "Yes, sir."

Appeased, Trevor hurried off to annoy someone else.

"I don't care much for Mr. Peterson." Harry said as they sat in the sun, eating Julie's sourdough bread and hunks of ham. "He's a wily one, he is."

Luke kept silent, glad for a chance to rest his aching shoulders from holding a hammer.

Another man, James Anderson, had joined them today. James worked with some of the men driving the plows. His dark blue shirt was always streaked with dust and sweat, his sallow face and arms black with dirt.

“Best not let him hear you,” James said around a hank of jerky, “best watch your mouth. I’ve heard tales. A body don’t want to go against him too much.”

Harry nodded wisely. “Truth to that too. But still, he’s a man bears watching. Things don’t be what they seem with Mr. Peterson.”

Chapter Six

A rapid burst of Chinese startled the three from their lunch. Another Chinese man, dark braid almost to his ankles, appeared at the edge of the railroad section. Trevor was there shouting, gesturing and then stomping off to a waiting buggy.

Harry moaned. "Now, that there's a sorry sight. They got them Chinamen in here to work. An' don't get me wrong, they're hard workers all of them. But only the one can understand the language—that one there..." he pointed to the man with the long braid, "name's Muchen Yu. He can figure out some, even speak a few words of English. But it's a fer sure trial to get them to do what I need."

"What do you need them to do?" Luke asked.

"Right now, I need them to take their picks and chop up the rocks so we can shore up the timber at the ditch. It's got to be flat, not a rock in sight. Then they need to carry the lumber to the site." Harry gave a mournful sigh. "It's fer sure goin' to be a long day.""

Remembering how he'd taught Billy when the little boy was young, Luke said, "Let me try."

Luke headed toward Muchen, stepping over the metal railroad ties to where the Chinese workers stood in bewildered silence. Pointing to his chest, he said. "Luke Morgan." He opened his palm and pointed at Muchen.

"Muchen," the man smiled, the dark eyes slits in his oriental face. He pointed to three other men and rattled off their names. Each one nodded a solemn greeting.

Luke had no idea what he'd said. Instead, he pointed at himself, then Muchen. He walked over to the pile of lumber, hoisted a board, and leaned it over one shoulder. Then he pointed to Muchen and the others. They each walked over, grabbed boards, and hoisted them.

"Where do you need this, Harry?"

With Harry leading the way, they followed Luke to where Harry wanted the wood.

The men jabbered in excited speech.

"Move lumber," Luke said and pointed to the small stack of lumber.

"Move lumber," Muchen agreed before speaking Chinese to the other men. They quickly moved the whole pile Harry needed.

Next Luke grabbed up one of the picks. Standing before a pile of rock, Luke took the tool and began to hammer away at the stone. He chopped into the rock where Harry needed to use the timber to shore up the ditch. Chips flew up and he worked up a sweat as the workers stared. After a few minutes, with Harry and James coming to watch, Luke had a flat area of ground.

"Break up rocks," Luke said. "Smooth." He ran his hand over the dirt patch, brushing stray bits of pebbles away until only a dusty patch of dirt showed.

Muchen spoke to the other three. Relaying his instructions, Luke hoped.

Again, Luke picked up a pickaxe and waited for the others to do likewise. As the men chipped the rock, Luke showed them how to take the small pieces of rock and place them in a wheelbarrow. "Move rocks out of the way."

"We work," Muchen said and bowed.

Each of the other Chinese workers took up a pickax. Rocks chipped into small pebbles and dust flew. Their excited babble filled the afternoon.

Harry looked at Luke with new respect. "Well, Luke Morgan, I'd say it was a fine day when the UP hired you."

***

One evening a week later, Luke met Greg at the Commodore Saloon.

"Whiskey," Luke told the man at the bar, taking the glass and bottle to sit at a scarred table.

Although work kept him busy during the day and often long after dark, Luke knew it would be impossible to sleep without a slug or two of whiskey. His mind would not stop long enough to forget.

Why, God, why?

Why Betty?

When he'd first met Betty in school, he hadn't been certain the shy, blushing girl would make a good wife. He loved her beauty, her sweet, gentle ways, but could she manage a family, a home?

As he filled and drank another glass, Luke couldn't stop the painful memories. The whiskey burned like fire in his throat and into his stomach.

I went to preserve the Union, but I should have been preserving my home, my family.

Billy and Hannah were too young to die. Their lives not even half lived. The servants. Luke had never bought a slave in his life but had sought out freed Blacks to work for him. *I wanted to give them jobs and a future.* To atone for the horrors they had faced in the South. It seemed such a cruel twist of fate that freed men should die at the hands of marauders. No sense. No reason. Just wanton violence and destruction.

And I thought the war would not touch our peaceful valley.

“Hi there, Luke,” Greg pulled out a chair beside him. “Coffee,” he told the girl who rustled up, “and one for my friend here too. Luke, don’t you think you’ve had a little too much tonight?”

“Whass i’matter?” his voice slurred.

“Do you think Betty would want you to keep mourning like this? From what you told me, she sounded like a fine woman.”

“She was.”

The waiter brought the coffee. Greg pushed the steaming mug toward Luke.

“This doesn’t seem like a good way to honor her, does it? Getting drunk every night? Sooner or later, Trevor’s going to wonder if you are up to doing the work. Drunk men don’t work as well as sober ones.”

It was the most sobering thought of the night. If he couldn’t work for the UP, where would he go? Luke reached for the China mug of coffee and drank. Gripping the warm mug, he stared at the scarred table.

“Guessssss...I didn’t think ‘bout that.” Luke sighed and took another steadying gulp. “Guess I better cut back on the whiskey.”

Greg nodded. “Probably a wise idea.”

“I just keep wondering why?”

"Sometimes there is no why," Greg answered in his gentle voice. "Sometimes like my Sunday school teacher used to tell me, life doesn't have to make sense. God's got a plan and we can't always know."

"What kind of plan would God have to kill innocent children? Billy and Hannah were still babies. I wanted to teach..."

Luke's throat closed tight. Hot tears burned his eyes. Quickly, he took another burning swallow of coffee.

The conversation had become uncomfortable. Just then Trevor Peterson and several of his cronies came through the swinging doors of the saloon.

Sure am glad Greg got me the coffee.

Luke edged the whiskey bottle toward the far side of the table. As Trevor and the men passed by, he and Greg both nodded but didn't speak. Trevor gave them a dismissing glance. Trevor and his friends took a table in the back and sat down for a rousing game of poker. Luke could only be glad Trevor hadn't caught him drunk tonight or on any other night.

Greg pushed back his chair. "Guess I should head on back to the camp. You okay now?"

Luke gave him a reassuring smile and lifted the white mug in salute. "Thanks."

"Any time."

"Greg," Luke looked over at Trevor, his slicked back hair looking oilier than ever under the flickering oil lamps. "Do you like him? Trevor? I don't care for him much myself."

Greg glanced at the back table and sat back down. Keeping his voice low, he leaned toward Luke and said, "Yeah, he rubs me the wrong way too. I've heard..." he looked around to make sure there were no listening ears close by, "well...rumors are that him and some of the top officials are up to something."

"Like what?"

"Funny business...but I don't know much about it."

Luke took a swallow of the coffee, burning his throat. He coughed and sputtered, aware Trevor and his men were staring hard toward their table. "What kind of..."

"I'll talk to you tomorrow," Greg gave Trevor an uneasy glance and left Luke alone.

A group of young boys peered around the swinging doors of the saloon as Greg hurried out. Seeing no one to dissuade them, they marched inside and scurried to Luke's table.

"Hey, um, mister," one boy with a ruffled mop of red hair asked.

Luke had to smile at the boy, with his gap-toothed grin showing a missing tooth. *Hannah was missing a front tooth the last time I saw her too.* "Yes, son. What's your name?"

"Timmy. Timmy Burns. Are you the man who made guns in the war?"

Luke nodded.

"An' now you're working for the UP?"

"That's right."

Another boy, even younger, a pair of ragged pants held up by tattered suspenders, eyed him wistfully. "Me da said you can make toys? Can ya?"

Reaching into his pocket, Luke brought out a small tin whistle he'd forged earlier. In his first few weeks at the camp, he'd seen how often the younger children had only rocks or sticks to play with. He'd taken to crafting small toys from scrap bits of tin or metal. Whistles and toy guns were popular among the little folks.

He fingered the cool metal and then handed it to Timmy. "Here you go."

Timmy's eyes lit up. The boy in suspenders licked his lips in greedy jealousy. "For keeps?" Timmy questioned.

"For keeps". Luke looked at the two boys standing behind Timmy. "Come visit me tomorrow and we'll forge you both a toy too. You can watch."

All three boys grinned. "How about a sarsaparilla?" he asked.

"Gee, thanks, Mister Morgan."

He waved the waiter over and ordered the boys a sarsaparilla, saddened by their cheerful boyish chatter. When they asked questions, he answered the best he could.

"They remind me of Billy," Luke whispered to himself as he watched them leave.

Suddenly, he wished he hadn't let Greg talk him out of getting drunk. It sure would have helped him to sleep.

And forget.

Chapter Seven

Labor Camp

Council Bluffs, Iowa

Run, girl, run! You best be savin' yourself, run!

Molly McGregor shoved a braid of fiery red hair off her shoulder and darted a look behind. Her green eyes narrowed as she peered into the twilight. Lips pursed, heart pounding beneath a yellow bodice, she stopped.

Anyone following?

Molly's breath came from a throat ragged and raw. A strangled sob slipped past her lips. She reached up to grab the torn collar of the yellow calico. One of the sleeves had been jerked from the seam. If she didn't step careful, the worn cotton would drop to the ground and leave her in tattered unmentionables.

Why would a man think he could take liberties? T'was it something I did?

Molly wished, as she had so many times before, that she'd never left Dublin. A wish never to be realized. Those days were long past.

Oh Ma, Da, how I wish you were here with me!

Life had been pleasant although poor in Ireland. Her parents were sharecroppers on a farm. Times were lean, then the potato famine made life even more unbearable. Working conditions were harsh, not something her parents wanted Molly and her older brother, Liam, to endure forever.

Somehow, Ma had come up with the money to purchase two tickets on a ship traveling to America. A land rich with promise and hope! At seventeen, Molly had bid a tearful goodbye to the only life she'd ever known. To Ma and Da and her best friend, Katie.

Once in America, Liam had found work on a ranch for a man named Trevor Peterson. It had seemed a blessing. Liam could help with the farming chores while Molly worked in the house, cleaning and cooking.

Although a touch annoying at times, Mr. Peterson had kept his distance. Molly had never been afraid of him in a house filled with other workers. Then came the terrible War between the States. Coming from Ireland, Molly could only understand what Liam explained to her about the fighting. Sure an' there were many confusing things about life here in the US that seemed foreign to her.

“”Tis the northern states fighting against the southern states,” Liam had said. “I'm not sure all the causes, but President Lincoln has called for volunteers. I've told Mr. Peterson that I'm going.”

“But Liam! What's to become of me?”

“Mr. Peterson says you are welcome to keep working here until my return. You keep earning an' when I come home, we'll try to find a wee spot of our own. Twill all work out, Molly, me girl,” he'd said with those green eyes sparkling, the dimples in his cheeks so like her own. He had kissed her farewell with promises to be home soon.

Except, he never came back.

Ah, brother, If you were only here to protect me now.

When news came of Liam's death at a place called Chancellorsville, Mr. Peterson—Trevor—had given Molly a choice. Set out on her own, or follow him to a place called Council Bluffs, Iowa.

Trevor had been given the job of Union Pacific officer, although Molly had never understood how he'd come to the position. He would oversee the construction and operations of this new railroad in Council Bluffs. A Labor Camp there would need many cooks and Molly could be one of them. It was honest work; well-paid and she'd have room and board as well. Although a cot in a tent filled with other workers hadn't seemed so fine once she got there.

Afraid to be alone, uncertain where to go, Molly made the choice to leave with Trevor. He made promises to marry her one day. With no other choice, Molly half-heartedly agreed, although for certain she did not love Trevor. The offer of a job had seemed a heaven-sent answer to prayer...until they arrived in Iowa.

Overnight, Trevor became a different person. Scheming, wicked and ready to begin acting as if they'd already been to see the priest and been wed. Molly spent too much time fending off his roving hands.

If only Liam were here!

But Liam was dead and buried. Gone and left Molly to defend herself among these wild, woman-starved men. Tonight, serving beef stew, she'd been assaulted once again. It had been more than she could bear.

Oh, Ma and Da! If I could only come home to Ireland!

Molly sobbed and clutched her ripped dress. Tears blurred her sight as she dashed across the railroad yard. Although she didn't know where she could run to—Molly only wanted to get away. Away from the crude men and their vile remarks. Away from the hands that pawed at her dress like that.

As if I had me more than a few dresses to me name. How am I to mend this one?

Where will I go? What will I do? The questions raced like cornered mice in her frantic thoughts. *If I could get away from here...away from him.*

Oh, Liam! What am I to do?

A pile of loose stones caused Molly to skid as she caught her breath and darted ahead.

Best watch it, girl.

In the twilight, piles of wooden cross ties, steel bars and tools made mysterious dark mounds. There was no moon, only a faint glow of burnt orange sunset still in the western sky. A bluish tint washed over the world. It turned everything gray and black. Looming over all the dark shapes were the railroad cars, silent and still for the night. Like her, the railroad cars stalled where they'd run out of track.

If only I had somewhere to go!

Although she'd saved a small amount, Molly had no idea if it were enough for passage back to Ireland. Or even how to buy a ticket home. There had always been someone older to see to such things, to decide. At twenty-seven, Molly often thought she knew so little of the world. That she was still as innocent as she'd been at seventeen, newly arrived in America.

She took a deep steadying breath.

Molly managed to right herself, annoyed at the rocks. She slowed to slide past a train car set off in a siding track. Past the train was more track still under construction. Molly had half a mind to follow the wooden surveying stakes of the track to come.

Where would it lead me? All the way to the Pacific Ocean?

The idea was so exciting, she began to walk faster, less aware. Too late, her high buttoned shoe tripped over one of the heavy wooden ties. Flailing to get her balance, Molly managed to wedge the shoe further under the iron cross beam. *Drat!* Molly yanked and pulled; certain she'd pull her foot off in the process. Although it was painful, she sat. Or tried to. The movement twisted her foot at a worse angle. Molly bit her lip to keep from crying out. There went a hope of unbuttoning her shoe to pull out her foot.

I'm stuck.

Oh, dear Lord, help.

Where was that man? Had he followed?

Molly bit her lip and pounded her leg with a fist, angered at not being able to free herself. "Help," she whispered, "help."

Another yank sent a sharp pain through her toes. The steel pressed down tight and unyielding.

Around her the black shapes grew more menacing as darkness folded over the world. In the black velvet of the night sky, a few pinpricks of stars shone. Although a dim rumble of sound came from the Labor Camp, there appeared to be no one close by. If only one of the workers would pass and help. One of the Chinese would be perfect. They wouldn't be able to tell *him* anything.

Molly allowed a couple of hot, piteous tears to drip down her cheeks. Not usually given to crying, she swiped her face with a tight fist.

"Take yourself in hand, Molly me girl," she whispered to herself. "Ya been in worse predicaments. Now, stop and think."

Although she often felt herself far removed from the Lord God, Molly knew he was just a prayer away. Hadn't Ma taught her well?

Please, send help. But not him. Never him!

He'd tried to have his way with her tonight. Molly had felt the flames of hell fire licking at her feet as his rough hands roamed over her bosom. Shame flamed her face as he tore at her dress.

Oh Ma. Da. I'm a miserable sinner. Black as the depths of hell.

The trapped foot began to ache. Pains shot up her leg. It might be June, but as darkness settled into night, a chill breeze blew over the dusty land. Molly's eyes watered from a stir of dirt blowing up. Shivers coursed up and down her arms. The calico offered little protection against the dew.

"Help!"

Molly called louder. Even if *he* heard, it would be better to go free than to spend all night out in the cold.

Out of the darkness, Molly saw a tall lean shadow walking toward her. She shrank back in fear. Tugged at her foot in frustration.

"Holy, Mary, Mother of God...help, help, help..."

The shadow came closer. Tall. Tall. Taller... then normal sized as he came close enough for her to discern his bearded face.

Bearded face. It's not him.

As the stranger drew closer, Molly was certain the face looked familiar. That she'd seen him before around camp.

"Are you in trouble?" he asked in a pleasant voice. "I was taking a walk and heard someone call out."

"T'was me," Molly admitted in a rueful tone.

"What seems to be the trouble?" he asked.

"Me shoe's gone and stuck under this tie somehow," Molly answered, ashamed to be caught in such a predicament.

The man didn't say anything scornful but squatted down to study her foot.

"I should probably go back for a lantern," he mumbled, "now that's it getting so dark."

Again, Molly knew she'd seen his face before. Where, she couldn't remember. There were such a lot of people working on the UPR. Swarms of them morning, noon, and night in the mess tents. The chaos in the cook tents with stoves blasting heat and pots crashing often gave her a headache. Faces blurred and passed like a spinning top. If she'd noticed him, Molly doubted she'd remember where.

"Well, let me see what I can do here," he said—unhurried, calm. "My name's Luke. Luke Morgan. What's yours?"

"Molly McGregor."

"Irish, are you?"

"Sure an' what if I am?" It came out more belligerently than she'd expected. Molly had heard enough imprecations against the Irish tonight from *him.*

I'm not about to take more from a stranger.

Luke took no offense. Instead, he chuckled. "Miss, have I your permission to touch your ankle? It appears your foot is wedged tightly under the bar. I may be able to twist it free."

Sure an' he asked to touch her!

Molly couldn't help the gasp of shock. A gentleman for certain. "I...uh...yes..." Her words sounded flustered. Of course, a true gentleman would not touch a woman without asking. Unlike some of the beasts she served every day.

What must he think of her?

Luke reached for her ankle and tried to twist the shoe free.

A squeal of pain passed Molly's lips as the pain became unbearable. Her toes felt numb, but her ankle blazed like the dickens. Just his gentle twist brought more tears to her eyes.

"Oops, sorry," Luke murmured, hand still tight on her shoe. "Let me try to dig a little dirt from underneath. Your shoe is wedged tight under there. How'd you manage this anyway?"

"I was running, not looking about."

"Hm." He looked up at her, concerned eyes questioning. Or so it felt to her. "It's not a safe place to be running in the dark. Were you being...followed?"

Molly ignored the questions. No way did she want to go into the whole story with him. Although she could see him studying the rips in her dress. Embarrassed to be caught in such a situation, Molly tugged tight to the ripped collar of her dress. She struggled to hold the torn pieces of yellow calico taut over her shoulders.

Let him think what he will!

Beneath her foot, she could feel his gentle hands digging out a hollow. Every few seconds, he would take her foot gently in his hand and tug to pull it out. Although it seemed time stood still, Molly's foot came ever so slowly out from under the tie. Prickles of pain stabbed her toes.

“We’ve almost got it,” Luke said and he bent to dig more. “Just a few more inches. Keep calm now...”

“What, am I some fractious beast just because I’m Irish?” Molly couldn’t help the snappish way she asked.

“Molly, me girl,” Ma used to caution, *“you’re too impatient by half.”*

“Oh, no!” His hand tugged at her foot again. “Almost got you free. I rather like the Irish. I’m sorry if I offended you by my question. Your Irish lilt reminds me of someone I knew...once...” His voice grew quiet as if he had to force himself to finish the sentence. “Our cook, Mrs. O’Shay. A finer Irishwoman was never born. I always thought her voice quite pleasing.”

Molly blushed, although in the dark she knew he wouldn’t notice. “I’m sorry. Me Ma always said to mind my temper. There’s plenty around here who dislike the Irish an’ don’t mind sayin’ so.”

Like him.

Luke’s calming voice and presence helped Molly to relax. Her fear slowly ebbed away. “May I touch your leg, Molly?” He asked permission again. “I believe if I lift your leg a little higher, I can twist the boot free.”

“Yes, of course,” His hand felt gentle and warm on her leg. Molly couldn’t help a slight feeling of attraction. Unlike *him,* Luke had *asked* to touch her foot and leg. Molly couldn’t help comparing his gentlemanly thoughtfulness with *him.* Such a kind man. Probably had a wife and children somewhere.

“There you go.”

Suddenly, Molly's booted foot was free. Wrenched and aching, but free of its prison. The feeling came back into her toes as pinpricks so sharp it took her breath.

"Thank you kindly! I thought I'd be stuck there all night." Molly took a tentative step and winced. The ankle would be painful tomorrow, especially standing at a cookstove all day.

Sure, an' that's what your trying to run away got you. More trouble and pain.

"You are welcome." He held out a hand to help her walk across the railroad section to firmer ground. Molly had never felt so cherished. "Do you need an escort somewhere?" he asked with a pointed look at her torn clothing.

Shame coursed through her body and Molly gathered the ripped edges of her calico against her chest again. "No, thank you, I..."

"Molly!"

A strident voice called from the camp. Molly's heart skipped a beat.

No. Not him!

"Who is that?" Luke asked. "Someone you know? The voice sounds familiar."

Only too aware of the anger in his voice, Molly could think of only one solution.

"Hide, please," Molly grabbed Luke's arm and shoved him toward a towering stack of wood. "Please, don't let him find you here."

"I have nothing to hide," Luke argued back, standing as firm as a rock. "Are you afraid of this man? Is he the one who tore..."

“Please, please. I beg of you, hide.” Molly couldn’t help the tearful pleas or the sobs that burst from her throat. She pushed at Luke’s solid shoulder urging. “Oh, please. If he finds you here, it will make it worse.”

Just when she thought he wouldn’t, Luke slipped behind a towering pile of wood.

Thank God, Trevor didn’t find him with me!

Chapter Eight

Why am I hiding?

Luke crouched behind a pile of lumber, unsure why Molly had insisted he hide.

I did nothing wrong.

While Luke's first notion was to confront the angry-voiced man he'd heard, he kept still. Waited. Perhaps Molly's fear was contagious, but Luke had no desire to challenge the angry voice just yet.

Not until I know what's going on.

Night birds and crickets filled the evening with a concert of chirps. The scent of newly sawn lumber tickled Luke's nose. He lifted a finger to hold in a sneeze.

Who is Molly anyway? Why is she so afraid?

Luke knew he'd seen her face somewhere around in the camp. Although he struggled to remember, he couldn't quite place her. There were swarms of people building the railroad and most of them were still nameless bodies to Luke.

Shivering a little in the damp night air, Luke moved to peer around the stack of lumber. He brushed against the wood and felt sawdust settle on the arms of his dark woolen jacket. He would stay to see who Molly feared. Stay to see if the woman needed help. Obviously, someone had taken advantage of her, torn her clothing. Luke clenched his fists, angered at the unknown person who would harm an innocent woman. Although he hadn't been around to protect Betty, he refused to allow another woman to be tormented.

It was hard to see on such a moonless night. From the distant camp, a few lights shone. The buildings of Council Bluffs were either dark looming shapes or glowed with feeble lights at random windows.

"Molly!"

The harsh voice grated at Luke's ears. A familiar voice. Luke tried to place who it might be. A second later, the man walked out of the shadows and came close enough for Luke to recognize a lean, sturdy man.

Who?

"I'm here," Molly spoke. "If 'tis any of your affair."

Hidden, Luke winced at the sound of the brave but frightened woman's voice.

"Watch your mouth, wench." The man moved toward Molly and grabbed her arm hard. Yanked her toward his body.

To Luke's shock, he slapped her hard across the mouth.

Molly whimpered but stood and didn't run.

Luke took a step forward, ready to come to Molly's defense. The man lit a match and touched it to the tip of a pungent cigar. In that brief flare of light, Luke got a good look at the assaulter's face.

Trevor!

"It's always my concern when my betrothed goes rushing off," Trevor said as he grabbed Molly's arm and pulled her close. "I expect the woman who will be my wife to obey me."

Although Luke had just a shadowy view, he watched Trevor pull Molly closer. He seemed to be kissing her. Or trying to.

A kiss Molly didn't appear to want or enjoy; she struggled away from him. Earned herself another slap and a hard yank on her reddish braid.

Molly cried out in pain.

Luke had to clench his hands until his nails bit into his palms. Although he wanted to rush out and defend Molly, he didn't. Not yet. If she truly was Trevor's betrothed, there was nothing Luke could do. By rights, any fights were between them.

I don't like this at all.

But Luke knew sometimes a person had to take a steady look at a situation to figure out a solution. Unlike many of the men he'd known, Luke did not go fists-first into a fight. Often, that caused more trouble.

It might make life even more difficult for Molly.

"I don't want you racing off like that again." Trevor's brutal voice continued to berate her. "You're to do as I say, when I say it. I told you that I wanted you to fix my supper."

"There was plenty of stew left on the stove," Molly said, with a little bit of vinegar in her voice, "I figured to have me a walk for a bit."

"Next time," Trevor ordered as he pulled her body tight to his side. "You ask my permission before you head off on a walk. You hear me?"

"Yes, sir."

Another slap, this one even harder. From his hidden position behind the lumber, Luke winced at Molly's struggle to stand upright. He couldn't help a small uplift of his heart at her bravery.

Molly and Trevor turned and walked back toward the camp. Luke waited, giving them a head start before he turned the same way, deciding to visit the saloon. If Trevor were occupied with his "betrothed" he wouldn't be playing poker at the Commodore tonight. Luke wanted the blissful surrender of whiskey in the worst way.

Frustrated, although he had no clear reason why, Luke passed by the Labor Camp. The odor of beef stew wafted from the cook tent, lit from within by oil lamps hanging from the rafters. Even this late at night, the tables in the mess tent were filled with men. Their raucous laughter and bawdy language filled the night. Silverware clinked against tin plates. Smoke wafted out from roll-your-owns or cigars.

As he passed the cooking tent, Luke glanced inside. At a black cookstove, Molly peeked up, noticed him, and pushed a stray wisp of red bangs from a flushed face. She'd changed from the torn yellow calico into a green dress that brought a sparkle to her mesmerizing green eyes. Although she turned away quickly, Luke couldn't help but notice her beauty.

Too beautiful for a man like Trevor Peterson. If it's any of my business.

Luke hardened his heart. What the woman did and who she married was none of his problem. Right now, he only wanted the blessed release of a night's oblivion. For his mind to stop the memories of Betty and the children.

Halfway to the saloon, Davis Jones hurried up. "Luke! Luke Morgan, wait up."

Luke stopped to wait for the chubby, bow-legged man to catch up. Impatiently. Davis could and would talk a man's arm or leg off given half a chance.

Davis was the civil engineer on the UPR. As far as Luke could tell, the man never stopped talking. Maybe even talked in his sleep, Greg had supposed one afternoon when they'd been joking about the balding little man who strutted around town, paisley vest outthrust with his own importance.

Although so far Luke had no cause to think badly of Davis, he had learned to be wary. There were rumors from Harry and some of the other workers that Davis's talkative nature hid a secret agenda.

It could be fact. It was no secret Davis was one of Trevor's top men. That the two of them were often seen playing poker or holding secret meetings in the caboose on one of the railroad sidings.

"I'm glad I caught you. I need you to sign these requisition papers so we can order more tin and iron. You can sign them and leave them in my office. I want to get them off in the morning's mail."

"All right. Where do you want me to sign?"

Luke could see his visit to the saloon fading fast. Especially if Davis started talking.

"I've left them on the desk in my office. You'll find ink, pens, everything you need. They're right on top. I've got to track down a couple of other people so we can get all those requisition forms out. Trevor wants them out pronto. Go right now."

From past experience, Luke knew it would be useless to refuse. He sighed. "I'll be right there."

Maybe if I finish before he gets back, I can avoid listening to him chatter on tonight.

Luke changed direction and headed toward the small office Davis kept behind the hotel. The UPR project had taken over Council Bluffs and set up offices wherever space was available. Offices were in a dozen makeshift places. Davis had a room no bigger than a cloakroom in a building once used as a warehouse.

The walls were whitewashed and held an impressive lithograph of Civil Engineer Theodore Judah, the man who had led many of the surveying parties to map out a route for the UPR. There was only room for a four-drawer filing cabinet and a massive roll top desk. A battered chair with a limp padded cushion completed the room. The cushion served mute evidence that Davis spent a lot of time sitting and looking important.

Luke sat behind Davis's cluttered desk and found the requisition forms with his name. He read them over carefully, not even bothering to look at the amount of coal, tin, or iron Davis had filled in. As Davis had told him once, there was no earthly way of measuring or listing the correct amounts.

"We do the best we can and use the supplies wisely," Davis had said the first time he asked for Luke's signature. "With the constant ebb and flow of the project, we'll use it all sooner or later. We just need to make certain we have the supplies we need without losing time waiting for more to arrive."

Unwilling to charge the government or any of the railroad investors too much, Luke had balked at signing his name. "That doesn't seem quite honest, Mr. Davis. If I were buying supplies, I'd like to know exactly how much I was buying and the cost. I wouldn't want to feel I'd been...cheated."

"Mr. Morgan." Davis drew up his body in a haughty stance, the worn paisley vest tight over his chubby stomach. "We're gentlemen here; we will not cheat the government or any investors. We estimate what we need and settle accordingly. If you are to continue to work for the UPR, you need to learn that is how we work here. Or do you wish me to tell Mr. Peterson you no longer wish to be employed here?"

Even though it felt slightly dishonest not to know exactly what he needed, Luke had caved in to Davis' demands to sign. When he asked Greg later, the other man had said it was all right.

"It's like a store merchant," Greg had explained. "He might not know whether he's going to sell three plows or four, but he orders five just in case. Sooner or later, he sells them all."

Taking a pen, Luke dipped it in ink and signed his name on the forms for things he would use in blacksmithing. They would be sent to release more funds for building the railroad. Luke read through once again to check over the amounts. It added up to a lot of tin and iron, but eventually, they probably would use it all. He also signed a third requisition form for more nails and screws, a dozen hammers and ten new pickaxes.

Waiting for the ink to dry, he thought of Molly.

Such a beautiful woman. Unlike Betty who had a fresh-scrubbed kind of beauty, Molly's was earthier, more rugged. That fiery red hair and shining green eyes more vibrant. Too bad she had to be tied to a man like Trevor Peterson.

He's evil and Molly's in danger.

Although Luke felt guilty for thinking of another woman after Betty, he couldn't deny an attraction to Molly. *Pretty little thing. Feisty too.*

If she was betrothed to Trevor, she was flirting with danger. Luke felt an uneasy knowledge about that. He felt an urge to help her. Somehow. But how?

Luke sighed. After blotting the forms, he stacked them neatly and put them to the side of the desk. Another set of papers caught his eye. More requisition forms signed by

Trevor. Curious, Luke glanced at the line to see what he'd said the UPR needed.

Moonshine?

Why would the workers need moonshine? The saloon did a booming business and as far as Luke could see, there was no reason for the railroad to be buying the men's beer or whiskey. Several merchants in town also sold alcohol of various types. Why would Trevor want to buy moonshine?

Looking at the amount of crates Trevor had asked for, Luke's eyes widened.

So much?

Luke had heard rumors that often moonshine was sold to the local Indian tribes to keep them pleased about the "iron horse" crossing their hunting grounds. And although he figured what a man drank was his own business, Luke felt a jab of suspicion.

Why should the railroad be paying for moonshine? Even to appease the Indians? Something seemed "off" about the whole idea.

"All finished?"

Davis hurried into the office and stopped Luke's pondering.

"Yes, just now," Luke pointed to his requisition forms. "I think you'll find them satisfactory."

Luke thought of asking Davis, but then thought better of it. Davis and Trevor were friends. It was better to keep quiet and ask someone else. Someone trustworthy like Greg.

Why so much moonshine?

Chapter Nine

"It's called the Union Pacific General," Greg said as he cut into a well-done beef steak on the white China plate. "It's going to be one of the most famous steam locomotives in the world. If this one goes off well, they plan to build more."

Luke stared at the drawings and plans spread across the table. Shoving away his own supper, he took in the specifications. Enough blueprints to cover most of the table's surface. A thrill of excitement coursed through him at the idea of forging some of those parts. "It's going to be a monster all right."

Greg nodded and chewed.

"How fast can it go?"

"When it gets up a big head of steam, as much as fifty or sixty miles an hour. It's going to be a massive achievement. Just think – it will make getting across the whole United States take less than a week. When it used to take months with a covered wagon." Greg's weathered face shone with excitement. Picking up his cup of coffee, he drank deeply. "I'm proud to be a part of it all."

Luke agreed. "I keep thinking how excited Billy would have been to know I'm helping to build the railroad. He loved trains. We only rode on one a couple of times."

The two men finished their meal with slices of peach pie, the cook's specialty, and more coffee. In a relaxed mood, Luke looked around the restaurant's dining room. Most of the tables had emptied, a few were occupied by railroad workers and a couple of ladies from the town. It felt like a good time to talk to Greg.

"Greg, I've been meaning to ask you something."

"Sure."

"You might not want to answer." Luke shifted on the chair, aware of people around them in the room.

"Then I won't."

Luke leaned over so no one could overhear him. "I was in Davis's office the other night signing some requisition forms and I saw something. Something not quite right."

"Oh?"

From the look on Greg's face and his sudden intense interest in the last bits of crust on his plate, Luke knew he'd hit a nerve.

"Trevor had signed a bunch of forms ordering moonshine. Almost fifty crates. Why would the railroad be buying up so much moonshine?"

For a few minutes, Greg went silent. "It's not the railroad business. It's Trevor, Davis, and a few others. They're getting the government and the investors to pay for supplies they want. They just act like it's for the railroad."

Although he'd suspected as much, Luke couldn't help the anger that flushed his face. He leaned across the table, tense and rigid. "That's illegal."

When Greg didn't speak, Luke couldn't keep the recriminations from his words. "It's also stealing. They're buying material and charging it to the railroad."

Greg shrugged, twisted back in his chair, and went silent for a moment. His dark eyes looked around the room as if searching for spies. Then he admitted, his smile shaky, "After I invited you to join the UPR project, Trevor and a couple of his cronies invited me to dinner one night. They told me about some 'not so legal' operations they had going on. One of them was buying moonshine with railroad funds."

"If anyone finds out..." the words caught in Luke's throat.

How could Greg condone this? Greg? A man I thought was honest.

"Don't you think I know that?" Greg hissed after another wary look around the room. "They asked me to join."

"Did you?"

"Absolutely not!" Greg took another drink of coffee and grimaced at it having gone cold. "I told them I was out. That I wouldn't say anything against them, but I wanted no part in it."

Luke didn't know how to reply. If Greg turned a blind eye to the scheme, wasn't he just as guilty? As a young man, Luke had always been taught to be honest and walk with integrity. What Greg suggested was that he'd turned his head on dishonest behavior. "Doesn't that make you just as guilty? Almost an accomplice?"

"I hope not."

"It's not right," Luke managed to find the words, knowing he sounded condemning, judgmental. "I can't believe you'd let men get away with illegal behavior. You, of all people. I can't believe you asked me to come here, knowing something like this was going on."

That was the worst part. Having Greg think so little of him and his integrity.

Did he think I would go along with such a pretense?

"I didn't know!" Greg insisted. "This all happened after you were on your way. I had no inkling when I asked you to come.

Trevor approached me after you had accepted my invitation and were coming. After losing your family and everything…" Greg had the decency to appear distraught. "Well, I didn't want you to have to deal with anything else right off. I'd hoped the men would be caught or stopped."

"By whom?"

Luke couldn't deny being annoyed for not knowing before he arrived. This was serious business—men skimming from the railroad. Although Luke had read enough to know that men named "robber barons" existed. They were men like Cornelius Vanderbilt and Jay Gould who had found ways to cheat investors and build the railroad. Although frowned upon, the men were not jailed or even stopped. Even Theodore Judah, almost considered a saint for conceiving the idea of the transcontinental railroad, had been rumored to overcharge his private investors.

"They asked me again the other day to help." Greg whispered while Luke was still trying to digest the news.

"Help how?"

Greg lifted a shoulder. "I'm not sure. Maybe in getting the moonshine to some of the Indian tribes or the men out on the graders. To be honest, Luke, I'm a little afraid this time."

"Why?"

"This time when I refused, Trevor threatened me."

For the first time since he'd met Greg, Luke noticed fear in his eyes, a wariness in the way he looked over his shoulder. When Greg reached to shove aside a plate, his hands trembled.

Luke didn't know what to do. His first instinct was to quit, leave. Although he had rented out the ranch, he was still a wealthy man. He could go where he chose, work at what he wanted. Or not work at all – although the idea was abhorrent to him. A strong work ethic had been engraved in his heart by his father.

When his hands were busy, either gunsmithing or blacksmithing, Luke felt a satisfaction hard to explain. Sometimes, as he began a job, hammering at a piece of iron, time fell away. As he pounded and shaped the metal a feeling of peace came over him. A calmness that filled in all the sad and lonely spaces in his heart. It was like being enveloped in a cloud of paradise. Luke knew he could never give that up.

"I want to leave," Greg said with an uneasy glance around the room, "but it's good money. And I'm not certain..."

"What are you going to do?"

Greg shook his head. "I sure don't want to get caught in anything illegal. But I don't know."

"Isn't there any way to alert someone, tell the authorities...if what they are doing is illegal?" Luke questioned, shocked at the sudden expression of alarm on Greg's face.

"No! You mustn't do that! Promise me, Luke? You won't try to figure this out. Just leave it. Don't say anything."

"I don't know, Greg. I..."

"Luke, please. You don't know what will happen if you cross Trevor or some of the others. Just let it be for now. I'll work it out somehow. Forget what you saw."

The idea of ignoring wrongdoing didn't sit right with Luke. It left an uneasy feeling in the pit of his stomach. But, for the sake of his friend, he gave a slight nod as if agreeing. Greg gave a shaky smile of relief, but Luke knew he couldn't promise to turn a blind eye.

I'll leave. If Greg wants to stay and be caught up in this injustice, let him. He's a grown man. I won't be a party to it.

It was only later, walking past the Labor Camp and seeing Molly serving the construction workers that Luke knew he couldn't leave.

If I leave, who will protect her?

It was a thought as unsettling as wondering why Trevor wanted so much moonshine.

***

Luke passed the Labor Camp cook tent as he had the past three mornings. Troubled after his conversation with Greg, Luke had taken to doing a lot of walking to clear his head. Although he usually had breakfast at the hotel restaurant or the saloon, the thought of running into Greg again made him change his routine. A few mornings, he'd grabbed a couple of apples from the local mercantile and a round of cheese for breakfast, then made coffee when he got to the shed with the forge. Harry or his wife, Julie, would see he got fed at lunch.

I don't know what to tell Greg.

Luke knew he was avoiding his friend and his growing attraction to Molly. If the truth be told, he couldn't make up a decision about what to do with either problem.

Why is she betrothed to Trevor?

The thought haunted Luke. He'd taken to walking past the cook tent just to look at her. So far, he hadn't spoken to her since the night he'd helped unwedge her foot from the railroad tie. Watching her was another story.

Ever since that night, he'd found himself watching her from afar. Those moments when he glimpsed her tossing wood in the wood stove, or dishing up breakfast were the highlights of Luke's day. The cute way Molly tilted her head, red curls bouncing on her shoulders, brought a smile to his face, lifted his heart. When she smiled—not often—a dimple formed in her right cheek.

One morning, he'd caught her taking scraps to a group of cats that hung around behind the tents. In such an environment, rats were a constant terror. Having cats to keep them under control was encouraged. Yet, most people didn't think to feed them. Or the couple of stray dogs that hung around. The dogs were so lean their ribs showed through. They hung beside the tables in the mess tents, whimpering when kicked by angry men, but too starved to leave. Often, they licked up the dirt under the tables for a stray morsel of food, a forgotten crumb.

After the men had left for the day's work, Molly took scraps and called the pitiful creatures to her side. Tenderhearted, she cooed and murmured to a group of cats milling around the tents.

Luke stood off to the side and watched as Molly tenderly stooped to pet a gray tabby and hand it a sliver of bacon. The ravenous animal snatched it from her hand and darted away. Two orange kittens came meowing for a portion. Molly found scraps of biscuit. Set down a plate of milk.

She's like Hannah. Another animal lover.

A cloak of guilt clothed him as he realized he'd thought of Molly and compared her to Hannah. *How could I? How can I stand here watching her, enjoying watching her when my family is dead?*

The agony of their deaths overwhelmed him as it did in unwary moments.

I've become fond of this girl. How did it happen? I can't let it happen.

Even as Luke thought of his betrayal, he noticed Molly had finished feeding the cats and tossed bones to two wiry terriers. She stepped back to the mess tent and looked around. Wary. Watchful.

Luke stepped back behind another tent flap out of sight. *What's she up to now?*

A whistle blew, signaling the start of the working day. Luke knew he was expected at the forge. There was a wagon load of pickaxes that needed to be sharpened. But he had to know what Molly was doing.

A second later, he got some idea. Molly walked out of the mess tent with a small threadbare satchel and darted away.

Now what are you doing?

Chapter Ten

Where do you think you're going?

At this time of the morning, Molly should be washing up the piles of tin plates and cups, peeling vegetables and preparing lunch for the next onslaught of men in the camp. Instead, she was headed in his direction—a direction that would take her to the center of town.

Although he should be headed to the forge, Luke darted inside a tent so she wouldn't see as she scurried past. Once he felt enough time had passed, he turned instead to follow Molly. He had suspected the night he'd helped her loosen her foot she was trying to run away. From Trevor, most likely. Today it looked like she planned to make another attempt.

Where does she plan to run?

He couldn't deny it was probably a wise choice to leave Trevor, but how safe would it be? Trevor did not look like a man who gave up his possessions easily.

Luke sped after her. Almost running, Luke hurried to get in front of her to block her escape. He grabbed her arm. "Where are you off to?"

Molly stopped short, green eyes blazing. "What the devil! Be off with you now. Out of my way!"

"I don't think so. Not until you answer my question. Where are you going?"

Molly glared at him, one hand on a hip. "An' what business is that of yours, Mr. Morgan? You aren't my keeper."

"You plan to leave, don't you?" Luke asked with a nod to the threadbare satchel. Probably had all her worldly goods in there. The thought caused him to wince at the depths of her poverty.

"And what if I do?"

"Do you have anywhere to go?" he asked. A grin tugged at the corners of his lips but he dared not smile at her fierce gaze.

Molly stood before him, dressed in a becoming dress of green gingham with a ruffled sunbonnet covering her fiery curls. If looks could kill, he'd probably be dead from the fierce anger in her green eyes. Eyes that blazed like sparkling gems.

"Do you have anywhere to go?" he repeated.

"No."

"Any money?"

"A little," Molly admitted. Her fingers gripped the brown satchel in both hands. A frown wrinkled her forehead, and she bit the corner of her lip.

"Then how would you survive? A person needs money and a place to go before they can get away."

Like a little girl, like Hannah, interrupted in mischief, Molly tilted her chin and answered in a childish voice. "I've a plan to go and I will. You canna stop me."

Now he couldn't help a chuckle. She sounded so much like a child bent on having her own impulsive way. "Molly, think this through, how would you survive? What would you use for money? Where would you live?"

"I'll figure it out." Haughty, she tried to brush past him. "Be out of my way now."

"Why don't you wait for a better opportunity and leave like a lady, not run in fear? You can leave at a better time." Luke suggested, unsure when that would be. "I could help you."

She needs a better plan if she wants to survive. I'd be the first one to help her escape from Trevor.

"What's going on here!"

Molly's face turned as pale as cream and her eyes widened in alarm. She gave Luke a stricken look and then gripped her satchel for protection.

Luke's own heart dropped. He'd recognized Trevor's fuming voice calling out too.

Oh, Molly, I'm sorry.

"What's going on here, Morgan? Why are you talking to my betrothed?"

Taking a deep breath, Luke turned to face his boss. "I didn't know it was against the law to speak to someone, Mr. Peterson. We were just having a conversation."

Trevor stalked up, grabbed Molly roughly by the arm and twisted it behind her back. She whimpered in pain, eyes glazed with fear. "I've told you never to speak to another man, haven't I?" Trevor yelled at her. "You never listen!"

"I – I – he spoke first..." Molly tried to lie.

"It's true," Luke agreed, saddened by not helping Molly get away from this man. "I spoke to her."

"Then leave! Stay away from her." Trevor hollered, face red with fury. "Molly belongs to me, and I'll thank you not to speak to her again. As for you..." he turned to Molly, palm raised, "I'll teach you to speak to another man."

Molly's eyes grew wide with fear, and she tried to shrink away from Trevor's upraised hand.

"Stop!"

Before Trevor could strike Molly, Luke stepped in and grabbed the other man's hand.

"Why, you…" Trevor spewed out the words and dropped his hold on Molly. He shoved Luke roughly away.

Before Luke could get his balance, Trevor pulled back his fist and aimed it into Luke's bearded chin. The powerful blow sent him reeling backward.

Luke stumbled at the blow, eyes watering. He might not go in fists-first, but he didn't shrink when it was time to fight. He drew back his right hand and punched Trevor in the cheek. Blood spurted from Trevor's mouth as he bit his tongue.

"Why you…" Trevor shouted some profanity and came at Luke with another punch.

Fists raised, Luke retaliated and landed a hard right punch to Trevor's cheek. Trevor got in another couple of sucker punches. One hit Luke's right eye. He knew it would be black and blue by the next morning. Another punch pounded straight into his mouth. His nose poured blood and one of his teeth came loose.

Luke spit out blood, nauseated as it dripped from his beard.

"What's going on?" Harry Miles hurried up along with the Sheriff, Todd Denver.

"Here now, here," Harry grabbed Luke around the shoulders while the Sheriff caught Trevor. The two men struggled to pull Luke and Trevor away from one another.

Neither man wanted to stop swinging but Harry and the sheriff pulled their arms behind their backs and forced them to quit. Trevor kept struggling but Luke, breathing hard, gave up.

"Now, what's going on here?" the sheriff asked with authority.

Later, Luke could never explain where the words came from or why he told such a massive lie. "This man is trying to interfere." He pointed a bruised fist at Trevor. "Molly and I have been seeing one another. She's ...with child." He whispered the monstrous untruth and watched as Molly turned so white, she looked on the verge of fainting.

"That's a lie!" Trevor bellowed. "Ask her."

Molly turned to Harry and the sheriff, but her eyes were on Luke. At any second, Luke expected her to fall over in a faint. If Molly's face paled any whiter, those green eyes would look like pebbles on snow.

What a horrid thing to say about anyone! I've told people she's a wanton woman.

"Ma'am..." the sheriff looked embarrassed but questioned Molly gently. "Was this man bothering you?" Whether he meant Trevor or Luke, the sheriff didn't say.

Suddenly, Harry spoke up. "If you want to believe someone," he told the Sheriff, "You'd bet your money on young Luke here. In fact," although Harry didn't wink at Luke, his sunburned face took on a rosy glow as it did when he told some of his tall tales. Harry could tell some whoppers. "I been witness to the fact this little lady's been seen in his company a few nights this week. If he says the lady's...well, I wouldn't want to doubt his word."

At this supposed agreement to Molly's being in trouble, the young girl burst into tears. "What would me Ma say? Oh, what would she say? You talkin' this way. Shamin' me..."

Before any of them could reply, Molly turned, still gripping her satchel for dear life, and hurried back to the mess tent. Her sobs echoed back and tore Luke's heart in two.

Oh, Lord, what have I done?

Trevor jerked away from the sheriff's hold. "Unhand me!" When the sheriff dropped his hold, Trevor yanked his rumpled blue suit coat back onto his shoulders. The look he leveled at Luke promised revenge. "You haven't heard the end of this, Morgan. And neither has that little..." the word he called Molly caused even Harry to blanch.

Trevor stalked away.

"Luke, lad," Harry started to say.

Before he could finish his sentence, young Timmy Burns came racing up the street. As he ran, his red suspenders kept sliding off his shoulders. Timmy grabbed the waistband of his worn knickers to hold them up.

"Sheriff! Sheriff!"

"Hold on now, Timmy, what seems to be the problem?"

Timmy's blue eyes were wide in his dirty face. It took him a few seconds of ragged breathing to speak. "It's Mr. Bennet, sir. Me Ma says he's dead. She went in to wake him up an' he's lying in bed. Dead."

Greg? Dead?

***

"Now, Luke," Sheriff Denver said as Luke towered over the man's desk, a sympathetic look on his careworn face. "Doc says it looks like your friend had a heart attack, pure and simple. Nothing else it could be. Wasn't a wound on the body."

"I don't believe it."

Greg was murdered. No one can convince me otherwise. He was murdered because he knew too much about Trevor's "business."

Luke paced up and down the sheriff's office. There was no way to tell everything he knew – not without losing his job with the UPR.

And what do I really know anyway? Just a few things Greg told me. Suspicions he had. No solid facts. I need facts. The only thing I know is Trevor signed a requisition order for moonshine. And how do I know that's not something he buys for some valid reason?

Although he and Trevor seemed to have made an uneasy peace in the past couple of days, Luke knew he was on shaky ground. At any time, Trevor could decide to bring in someone else to tend the blacksmithing duties. As if he wanted to ignore the whole fight and the lies about Molly, Trevor had shown up at the forge the next day with a new list of jobs. It made Luke uneasy.

What kind of game is he playing?

I'd like to leave. To forget all this terrible business and go. But then, what would happen to Molly? Who would protect her?

"Is that all you're going to do about it, sheriff? You aren't going to investigate anymore?"

"Why would we do that, son? Nothing to investigate. That's a fancy word. Folks tell me you came from New York. Mighty fine city, I'll bet."

"You don't suspect anything else...that Greg might have been murdered?"

"Oh, pshaw, no! Who'd have cause to murder a fine man like Mr. Bennett? Nicest fellow around."

Who indeed?

"I don't know," Luke admitted, "it just seems so unexpected."

The sheriff gave him a knowing look and nodded wisely. "Death can seem that way sometimes, son. The Lord moves in mysterious ways."

So do criminals.

Mysterious ways, is that why I'm here?

Luke had done a lot of thinking since the day of Greg's death. Praying too. In some way, he felt maybe coming to Iowa was God's way of putting him into place.

Maybe God needs someone like me to root out the injustice happening here. If He does, I sure wish he'd make it clearer.

"Well, we'll have a nice funeral for Mr. Bennett," The sheriff went on as if offering Luke some comfort. "He was a pleasant enough fellow. The UPR has offered to pay for the burying. Put up a real nice monument and all too. I reckon that's about all we can do."

Frustrated, Luke left the Sheriff's office with no idea what to do. He headed back to the forge, aware that he didn't want to get on Trevor's bad side. *I don't want him to find a reason to fire me. Not just yet.*

Greg was murdered. I know it deep inside.

"Hey, Luke." Harry came up leading a mule who brayed his annoyance at the whole morning. "This here fella needs some new shoes if you can get the time."

"Sure, Harry," Luke answered, not sure he could confide in the older man either. Since that day with Molly, they had not spoken about the events that happened. But Luke felt he owed it to Molly's virtue to tell Harry the truth. "Harry, about what I said about Molly...I wanted you to know it wasn't the truth. I was just trying to help her get away from Trevor."

Betty would have been mortified to know I'd told such a monstrous falsehood.

"I know that, lad," Harry chuckled, "since when have you had time to do anything other than the blacksmithin' for the UPR? An' fact is, I haven't seen you speak two words to the woman. But that Trevor gets my goat, he does. Speakin' to me like I was lower than a worm. When I saw a way to get back at him, Lord forgive me, I took it."

"Thank you. I know I shouldn't have besmirched Molly's virtue," Luke lifted the mule's left foot and began to pry the old shoe off. "But I didn't know what else to say."

"I think she knew that, lad."

"I hope so. It was a terrible thing to say...but I hoped to help her."

"You best be telling her that."

After Harry left, Luke yanked off the mule's shoe and began to mold iron to make a new one. As he hammered, he thought about Greg. There was no doubt Greg had been murdered. Luke didn't know who'd done the deed. But he knew who was responsible.

Greg had admitted he feared Trevor and his scheme to defraud the railroad. Then a few days later, Greg was dead of a supposed heart attack.

I'll never believe that.

As he worked, Luke thought about all the reasons he'd ended up here in Council Bluffs. Although not one to ponder long on God's reasoning, he wondered if somehow, he'd been sent here for a reason.

Could it be I'm supposed to find out what's going on and stop it?

Or to help Molly find her way?

I guess I'll have to find a way to tell her I'm sorry for what I said.

His face flamed with warmth. Luke knew it wasn't from the forge's heat.

Chapter Eleven

"Ashes to ashes, dust to dust," the preacher, in a black suit powdered with the ever-present dust, intoned as he stood at the head of the open grave. Bible in hand, he bowed his head and began to pray.

"We are here to commit the mortal remains of our beloved, Greg Bennett, back to the earth," Preacher Wells prayed in a loud but soothing tone. "Our hearts are heavy. We can never understand God's will here on this earth, but one day we will see His plan..."

Standing at the end of the grave, staring at the pine box holding Greg, Luke grimaced. *Why?*

Ignoring the preacher's heartfelt, earnest words about Greg's life, Luke stared off into the distance to the edge of the railroad track. An azure sky without a cloud covered the day. Birds sailed up and away from the always-present plumes of smoke wafting from the cook tents and the forge. A day fragrant with new-sawn lumber, faint whiffs of honeysuckle and wild roses. Just on the edge of the breeze, Luke sniffed the tantalizing aroma of fresh baked bread. God had never made a finer day. A day Greg would never see.

Even though Doc and the sheriff said Greg's death was from natural causes, Luke didn't believe it. Not for one second. It was no coincidence Greg feared for his life and then the next day was dead.

He must have refused to join Trevor's scheme again.

"This time I'm afraid," Greg had said.

It was the only thing that made sense.

As the preacher droned on, Luke remembered a conversation with Greg a few days earlier. As the locomotive engineer, Greg drove the train across the newly laid tracks to test them out. He'd been so cheerful as he waved to the children who lined up alongside the tracks. Every time he passed, Greg would grab the whistle and blast the air with a whirl of black smoke and a hearty WHOO WOO!

The children loved it, dancing around in glee. Their usually dull eyes would shine in delight.

Although he'd never married, Greg had cared about the little ones who milled around the camp. Worried about them getting enough to eat or being properly clothed. Even some of the smallest children were forced to work alongside their parents, filling wheelbarrows with rock. Their young bodies bent with work too back-breaking for even a man. It grieved Greg.

"What would the railroad do without you?" Luke had asked that day when Greg hopped out of the engine car to let a little boy climb into the engineer's box and tug the mighty whistle.

"Don't fool yourself," Greg answered, with a more serious tone than Luke expected. "If anything ever happens to me, they'll have someone else filling my shoes before night falls. I'm not irreplaceable."

On most days, Greg also operated as the fireman, since the train wasn't going too far. He'd shovel in coal, keeping a cautious eye on the array of gears and levers Luke couldn't even begin to understand. Greg knew his job though. He could stop that huge, hulking monster of iron within an inch of the last track laid. Luke figured not many men could learn skills like Greg.

He won't be so easy to replace.

Or so I thought.

Sadly, Greg was right. Earlier that morning, Luke had already met the new Locomotive Engineer—a man named Carmody. A skinny, sallow-faced man wearing a UP blue cap with pride, he'd sure shown up on "time."

I figured they'd at least get Greg properly buried before hiring a replacement.

Luke stared across the grave at Trevor with his fake mournful face. He and Davis stood beside the pine box, hats respectfully in hand, heads bowed.

You murdered Greg. I know it in my heart.

A ragged chorus of song interrupted Luke's thoughts as the crowd managed a few stanzas of "Shall We Gather at the River" after a fumbling start.

Most of the town and camp had gathered for Greg's funeral. He was well loved by almost everyone. Except the person who killed him. Luke could feel the massive crowd surrounding him, shuffling, coughing, murmuring in song. Irish, Chinese, common laborers, and the townspeople, including Mayor Willoughby. The voices were raised in song although some of the words were different in various languages.

As soon as Greg had been lowered into the ground, the mounded dirt shoveled back over him, Trevor began shouting orders.

"Let's get back to work, everyone. Time's a wasting."

The workers turned and headed back to the job site. The railroad must move forward. Grenville Dodge and the UP officials ordered it so.

Luke placed his wide brimmed hat back on his head and strode toward the forge. There would be more wagon axles to repair today. The construction crew had hit a rocky spot while driving out the mounds of dirt from the plows. One wagon axle had snapped, another cracked. Harry's men had managed to remove the axle and carry it to the shed.

Walking behind him, Luke noticed Carmody, the new engineer. Although the engineer didn't walk with Trevor or his men, it was obvious from the way they passed one another they were more than new acquaintances.

Well. Now. Isn't that interesting? That the new locomotive engineer, showing up at the funeral of the old, should be so friendly with Trevor?

Luke hurried to catch up with Carmody, to walk along beside him. "I guess Mr. Peterson hired you on, huh?"

The man's beady eyes narrowed over a beaked nose. His sallow face reddened, and he couldn't quite meet Luke's eyes. "Doesn't he hire everyone?"

"Yes, I suppose he does." The man kept his stride long, purposefully trying to get away from Luke. On his short legs, he looked like a banty rooster trying his best to strut.

"Kind of funny how things work out," Luke persisted, keeping up with the man, "you showing up right on time. I figured we'd have to wait a week or so for the railroad to send out a replacement, but here you are, like somebody had you waiting in the wings."

He tried for it to sound like a witty remark even though he fumed inside. *Your arrival is no coincidence.*

Carmody gave him an uneasy grin. Uncomfortable with the conversation? "Excuse me," he muttered, "I'm late for an appointment with Mr. Peterson." The man scurried down the dusty street toward the town.

Carmody's here because he knew Greg was going to die. That there would have to be a replacement. It's the only thing that makes sense.

From past experience, Luke knew hard work would be needed to quiet the grief he felt at Greg's death. He put his suspicions about Carmody to the back of his mind and headed to the forge. Maybe a day spent hammering out hot iron would ease the pain in his heart. If nothing else, he could pretend to be bashing Trevor's evil soul.

After a long hard day, sweaty and weary to the bone, Luke headed to the saloon.

How I wish Greg were here to stop me from getting drunk.

Because tonight, that was Luke's only intention. To get so drunk he could forget and sleep. Although not as grief-stricken over Greg's death as he'd been with his family, still Luke felt a heaviness he couldn't quite explain. Maybe, in some way, it was as if Greg were the last link to the life he'd known before.

I'm the only one left to remember my life before Iowa.

With Greg gone, there was no one left to help him remember.

Chapter Twelve

"Here now!" Molly struggled to push away the hairy hands of the man who tugged to pull her down on his lap. "Let me go."

"Aw, come on now lassie," the grimy man grinned with a mouth of rotten and missing teeth. "Give us a little kiss now, huh?"

"Let me go!"

His breath blew out, exasperated, and Molly almost vomited at the foul odor.

"She's a wildcat, she is," another spry, scrawny man joked. "Look at that purty hair and those blazing eyes. Bet she's full of fire and vinegar." The man went on to whisper a common phrase with evil ideas.

Molly tried to jerk free, shamed by their coarse language. They'd used words she'd only heard since coming to the camp. Words Trevor had to explain to her.

What would Da think?

"I hear tell she's a little free with her virtue," a third man joked, scraping a spoon across the tin plate of stew she'd served him. He took a bite. Gravy dribbled down his dirty face into a scrabbly, white beard flecked with remnants of his past three meals. "Best go easy there, Whit," he cautioned Hairy Hands. "Might be claimin' you as the Pa one day."

Molly's face burned with shame.

Whatever possessed Luke Morgan to speak such an untruth about me! Although she had a suspicion Luke had only spoken to save her from Trevor, the news had traveled fast through the camp. Women she'd only spoken to politely turned their heads. Some of the children she'd given cakes and cookies were not allowed to visit the mess tent.

I'm a tainted woman!

As if her anger had conjured him up, Luke passed the opening of the mess tent. Although he glanced inside, he quickly turned his head and hurried past.

Blast the man!

"Here now, give us a little peck on the cheek. Whit, let someone else have a turn." Scrawny shoved the groping hands of his friend away. He managed to get hold of Molly's arm and yank her toward him. "Come on, now, lovey...."

His next words were hollered toward the man who'd rushed in to jerk his hand off Molly's arm. "What the devil you think..."

Luke towered over the man, staring hard at his dirt-encrusted face. "Leave her be," he ordered the three men, giving all of them a fierce stare.

Taking Molly's arm gently, he pulled her away from the men around the table.

Whit glowered back. "Who are you to order us around?"

"The man who's going to punch your smirking face if you don't leave her alone."

Scrawny and his pal with the filthy beard shoved themselves to their feet, grabbed up grimy railroad caps, and left the tent. Although Luke appeared about to fight the stout man, Whit, the man's anger evaporated. Although he grumbled and spit a wide chaw of tobacco to the dirt floor of the tent, he stood. Then walked away with a backward glance filled with malice.

“I’m sorry they bothered you.”

Molly gathered up the dirty plates, unwilling to look at him. While she liked the idea of him protecting her, it was his loose lips that had caused the situation.

Him sayin’ I’d be visitin’ a man alone! That I’d allow him to …without bein’ proper wed! That’s unseemly. Wicked.

“Molly, I’m really sorry that I said what I did about you the other day…” He was unable to meet her eyes, looking down at the ground. “All I had in mind was to keep Trevor from hurting you.”

Even though she’d cried buckets of tears and feared for her soul, Molly knew he spoke sincere.

“’Tis all right,” she said in a quiet voice, suddenly knowing it was.

Someone was starting to protect her again. Almost as if Liam were still here looking out for her.

I like it.

Truth be told, it warmed her heart, it did. Even if he had protected her with such a shameful lie, still he’d done what he thought best.

“Well,” he shuffled his feet, like a shamed little boy,” I best be on my way.”

***

Luke headed again for the saloon, intending to have a drink, maybe two.

I won’t get drunk. No sense in that.

Even though he'd been determined the last few days to get as drunk as possible, Luke had sobered enough to realize a deep truth. Greg had cautioned him against getting drunk enough Trevor could find fault with his work. Luke knew that to find justice for Greg, he needed to keep his wits about him. Not be so falling down drunk he might be the next victim! Or give Trevor an excuse to get rid of him.

Still, it had been a long, tiring day. Beginning with Greg's funeral and just now having to defend Molly because his loose lips had caused her trouble. Luke could almost hear his wife, Betty's, scolding if she knew what he'd said.

"Luke Morgan! How could you imply that young woman was going to have your child? What a terrible thing to say."

I'm a cad. I admit it. I'll have to make it up to Molly somehow. Maybe let it be known about town I was drunk, talking out of my head.

He was determined not to get drunk. Still, a drink or two would relax him, help him sleep.

As Luke rounded the corner of one street, his Wellington boots squishing through a mud puddle, a man rushed out from a dark alley. It took a split second for the man to run behind Luke, grab his collar, and yank tight. Struggling to breathe, Luke jerked his hands up to grab the assailant.

The man held tight and dragged Luke into the alley. Three other men were waiting, all wearing dark burlap sacks with slits cut out for eyes. The first man released his hold.

"Hey! What are you..."

Those were the only words Luke spoke before one man punched a fist into his nose. A warm flow of blood coursed down Luke's lips. The metallic taste filled his mouth.

Another fist answered.

A second man twisted Luke around and punched hard in the stomach. Groaning, Luke doubled over, unable to get his balance before a third man landed a punch to the side of his right ear. Ear ringing, he stumbled for balance.

After that, the blows beat down on one part of his body after another. The pain became one large agony, each ache hard to distinguish from the next. The black eye or the gushing nose. The stove-in ribs or the throbbing gut.

An uppercut to his chin knocked one of his front teeth loose. Luke spit more blood, eyes watering and blurring. Blood sluiced from his nose, his mouth and one eye felt swollen almost shut. His black eye from the scuffle with Trevor had faded to a pale purple this morning.

Guess it will be black and blue again.

It must be the men who assaulted Molly, he thought in one part of his brain.

It can't be.

The men in the mess tent were rough, coarse. They smelled of sweat, creosote, and rotten onions. Whoever these men were, in their burlap masks, they smelled of bay rum and cigars. Expensive cigars.

Cigars like Trevor smoked.

Trevor's men.

"Hey, what's goin' on here?" Harry shouted from a distance. "Charlie! Stan! It's Luke! They're beatin' up Luke."

Luke heard his friends coming to his rescue. The men beating him dumped him on the ground. Luke lay there, panting and dizzy. By the time Harry reached his side, the thugs had run like the cowards they were. As Harry and his men pounded up, the others ran away, jumped a fence at the end of the alley, and vanished.

"Luke, me boy, what happened?"

Luke slumped in Harry's arms, beaten and shaky. His lips were bloody and bruised. One of his eyes throbbed from the pain. A sharp pain radiated from the pit of his stomach and every time he took a breath it was agony. Although he wanted to speak, no words would come.

"Here, lad, lean on me an' we'll go let Julie fix you up. You've taken a beating."

Exhausted, limp, Luke could only lean against Harry and Charlie and be led down the street.

This was just a warning I'm Trevor's next target. Especially because of Molly and my position here. The next time, I might be lying in the grave next to Greg.

Chapter Thirteen

End of the Line

Work Camp

Kaboom!

The explosion ripped into the sky, sending up a spume of black dust, dirt, and a shower of pebbles that rained down on the blasting crew. A group of Chinese workers scrambled forward with wheelbarrows, ready to cart away the larger rocks and shovel mounds of dirt.

Luke stood a respectful distance back from the initial blasting site.

"Quite a sight, isn't it?" Davis asked with a grin. Pulling off his wide-brimmed gray hat, he brushed the ever-present dust from the brim. "Just a couple of hours of labor and black powder and we can blow any mountain to rubble."

"It is at that," Luke agreed, wary around the other man. It had been something of a shock to have Davis greet him at the forge this morning with an invitation to go up into the mountains.

Uneasy, Luke had accepted, although he had his suspicions about this sudden jolly humor of the engineer.

I don't trust Davis any more than I do Trevor.

Although stiff and aching, Luke had managed to drag himself to the forge. He knew his bruised face was not a pretty sight. One startled glance in his mirror this morning told him that. Luke wondered at Davis's friendly behavior this morning.

If he was part of the scheme to attack me last night, why be so kind this morning?

Davis had borrowed horses from the livery and brought them to meet Luke at the forge. Although slightly stiff from the beating, Luke accepted Davis's offer. If the man wondered about the black eye or the swollen lip, he didn't ask.

Probably knows who beat me up. Or was he there himself, hiding beneath a burlap sack?

"I thought you might like to see how the workers are blasting through the mountains. You're the one who has to repair all the sledgehammers and driving spikes," Davis explained as they rode the distance to where the railroad tracks were stalled until a few hills could be moved. "We haven't had much chance to talk since you got here."

"I've heard the blasting," Luke made conversation as he settled a horse into an easy gait. Glad to be back in the saddle after so many days of standing and pounding a sledgehammer, he breathed deeply of fresh air. Most of his days were spent inhaling smoke. The ride toward the end of the railroad line gave him a chance to see the progress of the UPR.

Ever since Greg's death and the attack in the street, Luke had been extra cautious. Even though he'd thought again about leaving, he knew he couldn't. Not yet. Whether he wanted them or not, he'd found reasons to stay.

For one thing, there were Harry and Julie. He'd become good friends with the couple and their baby, Bonnie. Her delighted gurgles when he held her reminded him of little Hannah.

And another reason was Molly. *I've shamed her and I need to make it right. Somehow.*

The most pressing reason to stay, though, was Greg. If he left, he'd never find justice for Greg's murder.

Maybe spending the morning with Davis would open the door to questioning the man. Luke could only hope. *Davis knows more than he lets on.*

It took half an hour to ride up to the end of the survey line. A mountain of rock stood in the way of the train tracks moving forward. Luke knew from reading that when President Lincoln signed the Pacific Railroad Act, it had said the Central Pacific Railroad Company would begin building in Sacramento. They'd keep building east across the Sierra Nevada mountains. The Union Pacific would build toward the west from the Missouri River, near the Iowa-Nebraska border.

"I'd say the Union Pacific is right on track to meet up in the middle of this here country," Davis said with a note of pride in his voice as they sat in the saddles, watching the action. "We're miles ahead of the Central Pacific."

"They do have to drill through the Sierra Nevada," Luke acknowledged. Even thinking of the achievements he read about, he marveled.

How Billy would have asked a million questions about all of this.

Davis nodded. "We don't have a meeting point designated yet," he worried. "I've heard Grenville Dodge has some ideas. He's been hashing it out with the Central Pacific. Going to be a grand day for sure."

When they arrived at the job site, Davis led Luke to one of the two men teams who drilled the holes. One man would set a steel spike on top of the rock. The other man would take a sledgehammer and pound it on top of the spike. After each fall of the sledgehammer, the man holding the spike would twist it clockwise. It was almost like a dance, Luke thought, carefully timed, the steps sure and steady.

As the "spike" man twisted, the sledgehammer pounded. The spike would be driven into the rock to a depth of six to eight inches. One wrong move and the sledgehammer would land on the spike man's head or rough, calloused hands. The men drove the steel spikes into the mountain to provide a hole for the black powder.

"How many holes can they make in a day?" Luke asked.

"Oh, quite a lot," Davis bragged. "That team there—the freed Black, Randal, and the Irish, O'Flynn, can drill eight to ten holes in a ten-hour shift."

It seemed a lot of effort for a long day. Still, sitting in the saddle, breathing the fresher air, Luke found it interesting. Davis was dismissive of the men who did the job, but Luke admired their ability.

"I'm impressed with your skill," Luke told Randal and O'Flynn when he rode closer to them. "Until I came here, I didn't realize what it took to build a railroad."

Randal gave him a sullen glance, rage smoldering in his dark eyes and pockmarked face. O'Flynn, the Irish worker, nodded at the compliment. Stared at Luke's black eye and swollen lip. "Must have been a nasty scuffle, laddie."

Before Luke could answer, Davis changed the subject.

Deliberately?

"Get back to work, O'Flynn!"

"After the hole's dug, we fill it with black powder." Davis showed Luke the process, after one hole had been drilled to the proper depth. "Then one of the men drops a fuse down into it. He has to light it and run before it explodes."

Luke and Davis had watched from a respectful distance as O'Flynn dropped in a fuse, lit it with a match scratched into flame on his boot sole, and darted to safety.

Kaboom!

Another shower of rock and dirt filled the air. Randal and O'Flynn stopped to drink from a pail of water carried to them by a young boy. They each took a dipper of cooling water. After that, O'Flynn poured a dipper over his head, causing the dirt and grime to run in black rivulets down his sunburnt face.

Davis scowled. Made a derogatory comment about the Irish.

"After we blow a hole," he went on to explain, "the workers take handcarts to move the debris away to the fills." A group of Chinese had scurried forward the second the dust of the explosion cleared away. They began to load handcarts and wheelbarrows.

"It seems like a streamlined operation," Luke agreed. "No time wasted."

Davis grinned and nodded. For the rest of the morning, Luke and Davis watched two more explosions. Davis chattered away as always. At about midafternoon, he turned his horse back toward town.

"I need to head on back now," Davis said. "You can stay as long as you like. But, first, there's something I'd like to speak to you about."

An uneasy feeling stirred in Luke's gut.

Was this how it was for Greg?

Luke rode beside the engineer away from the work site. They pulled the horses to a stop beside a stream and allowed them to drink. Davis dismounted and went to fill his canteen at the water's edge. Uneasy, Luke stayed in the saddle. After filling the canteen, Davis hung it over the saddle horn. He walked around a few minutes as if stretching his legs after the ride.

"You know, Luke," Davis said as he lifted a dusty boot to the top of a nearby tree stump, "I feel like we didn't get off to a good start when you first came. Blast this dust! It's hard for a man to keep anything clean." Davis pulled out a handkerchief and flicked it over the boot. He gave Luke a conspiratorial wink. "Railroad building's a dirty business...in more ways than one."

"That's a fact," Luke spoke in as diplomatic a fashion as possible.

Davis stared off into the distance, as if searching for words. Not that words had ever failed him before.

Maybe he wants to use the right bait for me. To see if I can be caught.

"Around here, we work as a team or things happen. Like what happened to Greg. Greg could have joined us, but he refused. Nobody refuses and then expects good things to happen to them. Is that clear?"

Luke gave a wary nod.

Like the attack last night? Was that my warning not to refuse?

"See, people who won't play along with Trevor and the rest of us, things happen. Greg had a chance, but he let it pass. You understand what I'm saying here, Luke."

"Yes."

The engineer's pudgy face beamed. "Trevor wasn't sure you were willing to get into harness with the rest, but I said, let's give him a chance. That's one reason I brought you out to the blasting site today. To see if you want a chance to work with us. There's good profit in it. And at the same time...you'll be safe. You can see how easy accidents can happen; things can go ...wrong. People can be hurt. Killed."

Unwilling to speak just yet, Luke managed to tilt his head in a cautious nod. His fists clenched around the reins. He aimed for a calm attitude, but inside he seethed.

"I told Trevor you'd be willing to accept our offer to join us. Am I right in thinking that, Luke?"

Still aching and bruised from last night's beating, Luke wanted to punch the smug expression from Davis's face.

I'll never join scum like you!

Although his first instinct was to refuse, Luke knew he had to get to the bottom of whatever treachery was going on. If he didn't, there would be no justice for Greg's death. Investors and officials of the UPR would still be cheated and lied to. They would be forced to pay for non-essentials like those crates of moonshine. *I still don't know what's going on there.* Even though he wasn't okay with the plan, Luke knew he had to accept and play the role.

"I guess I could be persuaded," Luke agreed, half reluctantly, half interested.

"Good, good," Davis was all jovial good humor, "Meet me at the Commodore tonight at eight sharp."

What have I just agreed to?

Chapter Fourteen

"Hello, there, Molly."

The whispered voice behind her sent spasms of fear through Molly's heart. With quaking legs, she tried to keep her movements calm and steady. Holding a cast iron skillet of biscuits with a worn linen towel, she placed them carefully on top of the cookstove. Before she turned to face Trevor, she studied the eight pans of biscuits she'd baked for lunch.

Saints, help me.

"Hello, Trevor."

Why aren't you out botherin' someone else today?

Ever since the day Luke had spoken the untruth about her, thankfully Trevor had been scarce. Molly hadn't seen him at mealtimes—although truth be told, he'd only ever eaten in the mess tents when he wanted to talk to her. Or try to steal kisses or more of her affections. Usually, the likes of himself were too good for the worker's grub in the mess tents. He ate at the Stanley House or one of the saloons in town. Molly had only rejoiced those times, not been sorry to miss his company.

"Where's your swain gone?"

"He's not..." Molly jumped to answer, then stopped. If Trevor thought Luke would come to her defense, maybe it was a good thing.

Molly bit a corner of her lip, clenching the towel in both hands. *Me an' me fool mouth. Why didn't I lie?*

Although maybe Trevor had seen Luke ride off into the mountains with Davis this morning and knew he wasn't about to help her. Molly had to admit she'd worried a mite when she saw Luke ride past.

"Not your suitor?" Trevor sneered, stepping closer.

Molly backed away, her backside coming too close to the hot oven. She jumped forward, putting her body too close to Trevor.

At that time of the day, no one else was in the cook tent. She wished for some of the other girls who helped with the washing up or serving to come. No hope there. She'd sent Iris and Clover to pick up supplies that were coming in on the morning train. Most everyone else was out at their job, not hanging about the tent.

More'n two hundred men for each meal but no one around when you need them.

"I didna' be saying that."

Molly took a step to the side, easing away from the stove. Hoping to put some distance between her body and Trevor's without burning a hole in her skirt from the oven.

"You didn't need to." Trevor leered at her in a frightening way. Moistened his thick lips with his tongue.

The motion filled Molly with dread.

"I saw Morgan ride off with Davis. So even if he is mooning over you, I'd say he can't help you now. Since you seem to be so free with your virtue with Luke, maybe I'd like a little of that loving too."

Before she could run, Trevor grabbed her arm tight and yanked her closer. Molly's heart yammered in her chest as she felt his body pressed against hers. His filthy hand came up to touch her bosom as his moist, demanding lips pressed firmly over her mouth.

Molly's stomach heaved. Bile rose in her mouth.

No, no, no!

"Leave me be!" She struggled, but he held tighter, her strength no match for his.

"Aw, now, Molly, lass, let's have a little fun before anyone comes."

Molly never knew what possessed her, but she leaned toward the stove and grabbed the handle of a cast iron skillet. Swinging hard, she plunked Trevor on the forehead. Biscuits flew out like a yeasty explosion.

For one startled instant, Trevor stared at her wide-eyed. A second later, his eyes rolled back in his head, and he dropped like a stone to the dirt floor. He crumpled like a forgotten rag doll, arms splayed out.

I've killed him!

Molly wasn't sorry she'd killed him, but she didn't want to be caught.

Oh, like Father O'Leary back in Dublin would say, I wanted to sin and not pay a price. I'll be goin' to hell, if I've done murder.

Panicked, Molly knelt beside the body and put her trembling fingertips to the side of his throat. A slight, bird-like flutter beneath her fingers gave her hope.

He's not dead. Not yet. If he wakes and finds me here, I'll be the dead one.

I've got to leave!

There was no time to pack a bag. To plan. Once Trevor came too, he'd be in a rage. Molly had endured his rage before. Once he'd come near to beating her to death. It had been a week before she could drag her bruised body to stand beside a cook stove. To pretend nothing had happened. To lie.

Not again! Never again!

Outside the tent, Molly noticed Trevor's horse, a large bay with white socks, tied to a hitching rail.

I'll take his horse and ride somewhere. This time I will run away.

Molly took no chances. Hurrying outside, she untied the bay and pulled herself into the saddle. Iris and Clover, pushing a cart with supplies, called out to her as she rode past them out of town. Molly didn't glance back. With no clear destination in mind, she rode toward the mountains. Praying harder than she ever had in her life.

Where will I go? What will I do?

The questions hammered in her mind like a train clacking down a track. Over and over and over.

She had no money, no train ticket anywhere. Her few meager possessions were left behind in the tent where she slept with the ten other girls who cooked for the workers in the Labor Camp.

Oh, God—give me an answer.

Off in the distance, Molly noticed a man riding toward her on a brown gelding. Hoping to avoid running into anyone who might wonder why she was riding Trevor's horse, Molly tried to gallop away. The rider must have noticed her or the horse and turned to follow.

Molly was no stranger to riding. Even though they'd been too poor in Ireland to own a horse, there had been horses aplenty on Trevor's ranch. When she and Liam first came to

America, her brother had seen to Molly's ability to outride any other woman around. Molly knew she could outride women and most men. She tried now. Oh, how she tried to push the bay to a steady gallop. But the persistent man on the gelding raced closer and closer.

He can't catch me! I won't go back!

Leaning forward, Molly let tears slip from her eyes as she pressed the bay to gallop like a racehorse.

Hurry, hurry.

"Molly, wait! What's happened?"

Luke?

Oh, praise be—was he an answer to me prayer?

Molly tugged the reins and drew the hard breathing horse to a stop. "Luke, I didn't know it was you..." she said as he drew his mount alongside her.

"Where did you learn to ride like that?" he asked with admiration in his voice and a glint of respect in his eyes. Blue eyes, as dancing blue as an Irish lake.

"Oh..." Breathing hard herself, Molly took a few minutes to rein in her emotions and think about what she could tell him. Talking about the past would give her a little time to fashion an answer when he asked about the bay. "Me an' me brother lived on Trevor's ranch when we came to America. We often went out ridin'. He taught me, Liam did."

"Where's your brother now?"

Molly swallowed hard, feeling the grief about Liam all over again, "Dead and buried. During the war."

"I'm sorry." Luke sounded sympathetic, but he studied the bay with a look of curiosity. He waited a minute then asked the question she dreaded, "Why are you out here on Trevor's horse?"

A sob came unexpectedly.

"Molly? What is it? What's happened?"

"I've done a terrible thing." Tears streamed from her eyes, but Molly didn't try to stop them. In slow halting words she told Luke how Trevor had come into the tent and tried to make advances on her. Her face flushed with shame, remembering what Luke had said about her not so long ago. Molly had been a farm girl in Ireland. She knew how man and creatures mated.

Luke didn't take advantage of me, but he let others think he had. Why should I trust him any more than I do Trevor?

Although she didn't know how, she sensed she could trust Luke. Almost as she'd once trusted Liam. Even if his flappin' tongue had gotten her in trouble.

"Now, I don't know what to do or where to go."

Luke hesitated for a moment before he spoke, "I will protect you, Molly. As well as I'm able."

"How will you do that? Why? When Trevor comes to, he's going to be like a raging bull."

"Please don't take this the wrong way, but I think it's best if you move into my place."

Molly knew Harry and his crew had built Luke a small, one-room cabin near the edge of town. She'd also heard rumors that the Stanley House had asked Luke to leave after coming home drunk one night too many. Not that Molly saw that as a terrible fault. Her own Da had liked the bottle a little too much at times. And she'd heard the man was grievin' his family. Might be the man needed a wee dram to tide him through.

"An' what makes you think I'd be agreein' to such a scheme?" Molly asked, green eyes blazing.

Maybe I was wrong about Luke Morgan. The idea!

"You aren't safe from Trevor or those other men. If you are close, I can help you figure things out. Maybe you can get away, go somewhere else. We can figure it out together. I don't think it's safe for you to be alone."

"I've a cot in a tent with ten other girls," Molly argued, "not alone."

"That's not what I meant. You need protection from Trevor and other men's advances. If people think I'm going to be around..."

Molly pursed her lips and glared. "No matter what lies you'll be telling about me, I'm as pure as the day me mother birthed me. An' I'll not be havin' the rest of the camp think I'm a wanton woman living with a man an' not bein' wed to him."

He shook his head. "Molly, truly, I don't mean anything that way. We can have Harry build a room for you. Just so you're safe until you figure out what to do. Maybe Harry and Julie can help find you a safe place. If you don't want to stay with me, maybe you can stay with them."

"No!"

"You can't stay and let Trevor get you alone. Next time, maybe you won't have a skillet handy."

Molly turned Trevor's horse toward the mountains, her back to Luke. Again, her heart quailed. *Where will I go? What will I do?*

"Molly, listen to reason." Luke rode beside her. "I have no intention of taking advantage of you. I'm just offering you a safe haven. Until you can figure out what to do."

As she rode, Molly realized Luke was much like Liam—offering her protection. And truly, what other choice did she have? When Trevor came to, he'd be angrier than he'd ever been. Not only had she hit him, but she'd taken his horse. Molly had been in America long enough to know horse thieving meant people hung—even women!

Luke didn't speak again but rode quietly behind her. Molly could hear the steady plodding of his horse. Although it pained her to admit it, she knew she had no choice. If she stayed in the tent, no one could help her if Trevor came to get vengeance. He might hurt one of the other girls too.

"All right, I'm beholden to you. But so, help me, if you try to take any liberties, I'll hit you with a fry pan like I did Trevor."

He grinned but didn't say anything else.

They rode back to the cook tent. Molly let him go inside first to see if Trevor had recovered...or died.

Truth be told, Molly couldn't decide which would be the best outcome.

Chapter Fifteen

"No one here." Luke came out after a quick look around. "Pack your things quickly and I'll take you to the cabin. I have some..." He seemed to hesitate like he might be searching for words. "business tonight. A meeting. You can get settled while I'm gone."

It didn't take long to pack up her belongings, including one cherished gift Liam crafted for her before the war. A small gold locket on a chain. Inside, was a precious lock of Liam's auburn hair. Molly put it around her neck and tucked it beneath the collar of her dress.

They left Trevor's horse tied to a pole of the mess tent.

At least I won't be hung for horse thievin'.

Luke's cabin was more cramped than Molly realized.

An' me agreein' to such a scheme?

She hesitated at the door, looking at a small bed in one corner, a tidy dresser with an oil lamp and one straight-backed chair beside the black Franklin stove. On top of the dresser, she noticed a daguerreotype in a black velvet case.

"You can have the bed," Luke said as he placed her satchel on top of the brown army blanket. "I'll make a pallet on the floor. You can go ahead and put your things in one of the drawers. I didn't bring a lot with me."

"When will you be back?"

A worried look crossed his face. He quickly replaced it with a reassuring smile.

"I'm not sure."

Molly wondered where he planned to go but thought it best not to ask. Not when she had a more pressing need to be taken care of.

"Can you do me a wee favor? I'll be findin' a way to pay you for your troubles."

"That's not necessary."

""Tis," Molly argued, "I want a gun. And I'm expectin' I'd need to learn how to shoot."

To Molly's relief, he took her seriously. "A good idea," he agreed. "I can make you one that's small and handy. With a bit of a kick, like you," he teased. "Just as soon as I can. But now, I've got that meeting to get to. Make yourself at home."

The door closed behind him. Molly stared around at the small room, overwhelmed. She sat on the bed, little more than a nicer cot than the one she had in the tent, and sighed.

What would Ma an' Da think of my predicament? Or Father O'Leary?

Molly knew she couldn't go back to the tent. Not if Trevor were lying in wait to get revenge. Next time, she might not have a handy weapon ready. Somehow, some way, she would have to figure out how to get away. As far away from Trevor Peterson and Council Bluffs as she could travel.

She shuddered, remembering Trevor's groping hands on the front of her dress. His wet, bruising lips coming down hard on her mouth. He would never have the chance again.

I'll kill him first.

***

As usual this time in the evening, the Commodore Saloon bustled with life and activity. A haze of smoke filled the air along with a tinkle of the piano keys, played by a dark-faced man named Moses. A variety of voices talked, laughed, or argued from several poker games going on at the tables covered in green felt. Workers stood beside the bar, drowning their troubles in beer. A not unpleasant clink of glasses, boot shuffling and the sputtering of oil lamps added to the din.

As Luke pushed through the swinging doors, he saw Davis and Trevor sitting at a table near the back of the crowded room. Luke hid a grin as he noticed the reddened knot on Trevor's forehead.

Molly sure had good aim! She conked him a good one.

Luke made his way past other tables, sidestepping a tipsy old timer who must have one too many drinks.

"S'cuse me, s'cuse me," the bearded man muttered as he shoved past Luke. Before he could clear the swinging saloon doors, the old man dropped into a chair. Within seconds his shaggy head hit the table and his snores added to the noise.

A saloon girl in a gaudy yellow dress fringed with feathers and sequins hurried to Luke's side. Her rouged face showed more years than she'd admit. A sight that filled Luke with sympathy. *Not a bad looking woman, wonder how she ended up in this sordid life?*

"I'll have whiskey," Luke said as he pulled out a chair and sat across from Davis.

Although Luke had supposed Davis and Trevor were friends, the men sat apart, their disdain for one another obvious. So maybe the partners in crime were not as chummy as they appeared.

I sure wish Greg were here to talk to now.

"Luke," Davis' chubby face beamed as if he'd personally engineered the invitation. "I knew you'd come. You strike me as a man who goes after what he wants."

Across the table, Trevor glared with an unreadable expression. "Davis tell you what we want?"

Luke waited for Priscilla, the saloon girl, to place his glass of whiskey in front of him. "Bring the bottle," he told her. When she'd walked away, he looked at Trevor and then Davis. "He didn't tell me exactly, no. Just said I'd be wise to listen to your plan. I'm listening."

At a nod from Trevor, Davis sat forward and folded his pudgy hands around a glass of beer. "We've got an important plan for you, Luke. One I hope you'll be agreeable to. You know who Grenville Dodge is, of course."

Luke nodded, took a swallow of whiskey.

Of course, he knew who Grenville Dodge was. Dodge had served under General Grant during the war. An excellent engineer, he'd once built a bridge 14 feet high and 710 feet long across the Chattahoochee River. *While others might have prolonged the project, Dodge managed the feat in just three days.* Later, he'd become the chief engineer for the Union Pacific. The newspapers couldn't print enough about the illustrious man or his deeds.

"In a few days, Mr. Dodge and some of his people will be visiting here. They are curious to see how things are progressing. Which leaves us with a bit of a dilemma."

Davis glanced at Trevor to see if he was explaining things correctly. Trevor picked up a rag from the table and pressed it against the knot on his forehead. The pungent odor of witch hazel tickled Luke's nose. Again, he fought to control a grin.

"You get hurt, Mr. Peterson?" Luke couldn't help asking, wanting to see how the man would answer.

"Ran into a door," Trevor muttered the lie. "Have a splitting headache. Davis, tell him what we need."

"What we need from you, Luke, is a secret hiding place. With Mr. Dodge visiting, let's just say we are going to need to transport some items with a little more discretion than usual. We need some modifications made to one of the railroad cars. A very minor job."

Luke glanced from man to man. "What kind of items?"

"Crates," Trevor snapped, pressing the rag to the knot. He winced. "We need you to do the ironwork to make pieces that will look natural. They will conceal a space to hide about fifty crates. Without looking as if anything is different with the railroad car."

"Mind if I ask crates of what?"

"It depends on if you are agreeing to do it," Davis said with a hint of malice in his voice.

Luke swallowed the rest of the whiskey in the glass. He picked up the bottle and poured another drink. "Said I'd meet you here, didn't I?"

Davis glanced at Trevor. Trevor studied Luke; eyes half closed. Finally, Trevor gave a slight nod.

"Moonshine," Davis answered, "fifty crates for now. Can you make some type of hiding place in the baggage car that won't look too suspicious to men who know the specifications of each piece of UP equipment? You will be paid well, of course."

Luke had no need of money. And he certainly didn't aim to take money for an illegal activity. What would Grenville Dodge think of such a shady operation using the UP? As far as Luke knew, Dodge seemed honest. General Grant had always thought so.

"It shouldn't be too difficult," Luke answered, already seeing how it could be done. "It would be an easy matter to take iron and craft it into several small holding spots. Less obvious to carve off a few inches here and there than to create one big holding spot that would be easily noticed. It's just a matter of fooling the eye."

Luke had often crafted hidden safes and hidey-holes for his neighbors. After the war's beginning, many had worried about hiding their valuables in case of attack.

"Good, good," Davis rubbed his hands together. "Ah, here comes Bruce, another member of our team."

Luke turned to see Bruce Scott, the telegraph operator, joining them at the table. He carried a foaming glass of beer and glanced at the girl in the yellow satin gown with a confused expression on his face.

"What happened to Aura Lee?" he asked as he pulled out a chair and sat down. "That one there just spilled beer all over my uniform." He brushed at a damp patch on the front of his brown, Western Union jacket. "I'd just got Aura Lee to know how I liked things."

Davis shrugged, "You know how fast saloon girls come and go around here. They don't stay long."

Bruce looked around, puzzled.

Luke understood the feeling. Go where? he wanted to ask. Until Bruce mentioned Aura Lee, Luke hadn't remembered the other saloon girl. A fiery redhead, although her eyes were dull and didn't give off a sparkle as Molly's did.

Now that he thought about it, every time he'd been in the Commodore, there seemed to be a new girl. He'd get used to one serving his whiskey, then a few days later, there would be a new one. He too remembered Aura Lee as very efficient. Ugly as a mud fence, but capable and neat.

"Still," Bruce mourned, "kind of sad how fast they go. Wish they could stick around a little longer. Seems to me we could keep them on until..."

"You fool," Davis snapped, "keep your mouth shut. You talk too much."

Luke didn't have to pretend to notice the angry nod Davis gave toward him.

"When do you want me to start working on this...job?" Luke asked as if he wasn't suspicious at all.

There was something going on about the saloon girls Davis didn't want Bruce to spill.

What?

"As soon as possible," Davis said. "Mayor Willoughby had a telegram from Mr. Dodge yesterday. He wants things taken care of well before he arrives."

The mayor too? He knows and condones all this deception?

Luke took a casual swallow of whiskey and nodded.

Trevor. Davis. Bruce. The mayor. If they're all in cahoots to rob the railroad and use it for their schemes, how widespread is it?

Who else is part of this? Are there no honest men working on the UP?

Chapter Sixteen

Once Luke left, Molly hurried to fold her few possessions in the bottom drawer of the dresser. Thinking about Luke's return, she made up a pallet for him on the floor with a couple of spare blankets she found in another drawer.

Sure an' it would be a hard sleeping spot. Molly sighed. She still couldn't decide if this fool idea was good or bad. It would keep Trevor from finding her for a few days, but eventually he'd learn she'd moved from the women's tent. He'd been watching to catch her like a spider with a fly.

Furious for sure.

Molly had seen the fight between Trevor and Luke. One of the other girls had told her Luke had also been beaten in an alley a few days before. Molly couldn't help wondering if it was Trevor's way of getting back at Luke. Luke's face still showed signs of bruising and one eye looked to be puffy.

An' me caught in the middle.

She'd have to show up for work the next morning or not get paid. Molly tried to think of another job she might do, but nothing came to mind.

Sure an' I'm not so desperate I'll ask for work at the Commodore. The very idea of wearing a low-cut, flimsy dress showing her knees filled Molly with shame. *I've enough sins counted to me name already.*

Molly built up a small fire in the wood stove, made a pot of coffee and tried to drink a cup. Luke had very few supplies. Nothing to make a meal except for a hardened hunk of bread. Molly was hungry enough to eat it, staring nervously out the window as the night deepened. Every sound from outside caused her to jump, sure it was Trevor.

After a while, she lit the oil lamp, pulled her cotton nightgown from the drawer, and dressed for bed. She'd just pulled off her petticoat and loosened her chemise when she saw a man's shadowy shape through the un-curtained window.

Luke or Trevor?

Molly wrenched the nightgown over her head, blew out the lamp, and dove into the bed. Just as she jerked the coarse army blanket up to her chin, the cabin door creaked open. She shut her eyes and feigned sleep.

Please, please, please.

A man walked inside, shut the door quietly and lit a match. Molly heard the scritch, saw the tiny flame waver around the room. She dared not breathe or move. Even her heart felt frozen with a tense waiting. The light went out and she heard—it had to be Luke—shrugging off his coat and tugging off his boots. After a few minutes, she heard him settling on the floor, trying to get comfortable. A sigh escaped his lips.

Luke for sure.

Molly lay in bed, the fear melting slowly out of her limbs. The rustling of Luke trying to settle to sleep felt comforting. He would not try to hurt her or force himself on her. It was almost like sharing a room with Liam again.

Staring into the darkness, Molly let herself relax. She thought back to the first moment she'd met Luke, when he helped her get unstuck from the railroad tie.

A gentleman, for sure. He'd ask permission before so much as touching her foot! Something Trevor had never done. Trevor thought nothing of mauling her in the most indecent ways. Touching the private parts of her body as if he had every right – the rights of a husband, proper wed.

Tonight, Luke had gone to bed. Quietly. Kind enough not to light a glaring lamp in her eyes. A warmth spread through Molly's heart. It made her feel cherished. Treated in a kind-hearted way Da had always loved Ma.

In the darkness, Molly smiled.

***

Luke tried to sleep but the solid, unyielding boards between the thin layer of blankets made it impossible. He tried to remember the last time he'd slept this rough. Maybe during the war, when they had to camp out in the woods. He'd spent many a night on the hard, cold ground with just a thin blanket for comfort. Thinking back, the ground had been a bit more comfortable than this hard plank floor.

A fleeting remembrance of the soft, feather bed he'd shared with Betty taunted at the edge of his memory.

Oh, Betty.

Betty's smile could charm any man out of his boots. Her cheerful disposition, twinkling blue eyes and sweet ways had turned Luke's head way back in the one room schoolhouse. Although he'd first proposed marriage at age eight, Betty had wisely insisted they wait until they were of age. Marrying her was a decision Luke had never regretted. He'd often thought how he and Betty were like twin halves of an apple—his favorite fruit. Together, they made one perfect whole.

Did I cherish my life with Betty and the children enough?

A rustle from the bed drew his attention.

What would Betty think about Molly?

Luke thought of the meeting he'd just had with Trevor and Davis. Cushioning his neck on one arm, he forced his eyes closed. Sleep. Sleep.

What will Trevor do or say if he knows I've taken Molly in?

Luke vowed to watch himself and his surroundings. To be extra cautious. Taking deep breaths, he willed himself to sleep. To rest. Tomorrow would be another long day. He'd have to tread carefully with Trevor. And find a way to create those hiding places in the baggage car. As always when he began a project, his mind probed at the possibilities, the specifications he'd need to sketch. Despite the illegal aspect, his mind eagerly sorted out the details. The hidden hinges, the subtle lines of ironwork that would draw the eye away. It was always a challenge to mold iron to a certain angle.

Why am I doing this?

Again, his mind raced around all the reasons he needed to get to the bottom of Trevor's scheme. Sleep eluded him. Another hour passed. After a while, Luke just lay on the floor, planning the project in his mind.

A sudden squeak of the bed made him wonder.

"Molly?" he whispered, "you awake?"

A hesitant "no" came from the bed.

Luke sat up. Stretched. Too fidgety to lie still any longer. "I can't sleep either. I was thinking. Since you want a gun and want to learn to shoot, why don't we practice some now?"

"Now? Sure an' it's a fool idea. 'Tis the middle of the night."

"Why not?" Luke tugged on his leather boots. He didn't need the lamp to find his old Army Colt and holster buried beneath a pile of blue trousers in the dresser. "I'm far enough away from town and the camp, no one will question gunfire. Let's go out and practice. Do you know how to shoot at all?"

Without waiting for an answer, he lit the oil lamp. Carrying the lamp by the handle, he walked to the door.

Molly grumbled, but by the time he reached the door, she had gotten out of bed. In her long white nightgown, those red curls draped over her shoulders, she took Luke's breath away. He swallowed hard and forced himself to empty the bullets from the gun's cylinder.

How can I even look at another woman after losing Betty?

"Grab up my jacket," he said in a gruff voice, "it's a little chilly out here."

Luke walked a short distance from the cabin. A couple of bales of hay sat beside a stack of lumber. "Do you know anything about shooting?" He asked again. "How to hold and aim a gun?"

"Sure an' you think I'm daft?" Molly argued, holding out her hand for the Colt.

Just to test her, Luke kept his hand on the grip and held the empty gun out toward her. As he'd figured she would, Molly grabbed the barrel and tried to pull it out of his hand.

"No," he said gently, keeping a firm hold on the gun. "Never grab a gun by the barrel. What if it had been loaded? It might have discharged right into your chest."

Molly gave him an annoyed huff and dropped her hand. "An' sure and you'll show me the right way?"

Luke took her hand, almost as he would have Hannah's, and placed it firmly around the gun's grip. "You hold it here, then move your finger down to the trigger..." He lifted Molly's right finger and placed it on the trigger. "After that you look down the barrel, sight where you want to aim and try to get the muzzle pointed in that direction. Then pull back on the trigger and shoot. Go ahead and practice. It's not loaded."

For just a moment, Luke didn't want to release his hold on her hand. A small, warm hand cupped beneath his own. An indescribable feeling crept into his heart—almost like the first time he'd felt sparks between himself and Betty. A little electrical snap burned the tips of his fingers. Molly released the Colt and Luke caught it before it hit the ground.

Molly jumped back, startled. *Had she felt it too?*

"Tis enough of a lesson for tonight," she mumbled and hurried back to the cabin, his jacket clenched around her shoulders.

Luke could only stand in wonder.

What just happened?

Chapter Seventeen

"Drat, you blasted kindling, catch!" Molly bent over the cold, yawning mouth of the oven and tossed in another match. Each morning it was a battle to get a fire started and food cooking to fill the hungry mouths of the workers. Finally, a spark bit into a wood chip as she waved her green apron gently to give it some air. The chips caught and flames snapped into the kindling she'd stacked in a teepee shape. Soon, the fire was hot enough to add more sticks of wood.

Molly rubbed her chilled hands together and began to bang the cast iron skillets into place on the stove's wide top. A grin flickered across her face when she thought of bashing Trevor's smug face the day before.

Sure an' I'm a sinner enjoyin' the misfortune I caused another.

"Molly," Clover came up with a basket of eggs and began to crack them into the skillets, "How many should we scramble this morning?"

"Start off with three dozen," she answered, pulling out the ingredients for a batch of biscuits. "We'll need more but only a few men will show up early."

So, another day began. While it had been confusing at first, Molly had soon gotten into a routine with cooking the three squares the UP granted its workers. Iris and Clover, though young, could be depended upon to help with the first round of hungry workers.

After that, there were another group of girls who did only the washing up—an endless round of tin plates, cups, and silverware. They would no sooner get the breakfast dishes washed up when it was time to stack them for the noon meal.

Afternoons, they'd wash up and stack for dinner. Thankfully, they could cook in the camp and not have to move so often right now. Once the tracks were laid a little farther out, they'd pull up stakes and move all the tents again. Molly had gotten used to following the railroad tracks west.

As the chief cook, Molly totaled up their supplies, kept careful control of how much food they used each meal and came up with a weekly plan. It was also Molly who assigned the jobs each girl did. Once they finished breakfast, they might have a wee spot of time before starting to wash and peel vegetables or put on a stew for the noon meal. There was always bread or biscuits to bake.

This morning, as she fried up slices of ham to go with the eggs and biscuits, Molly kept a watchful eye for Trevor. He hadn't shown up, filling her with equal parts curiosity and dread.

Maybe he's got a headache this morning.

Usually, even if he didn't come inside the mess tent for a meal, Molly might feel an uneasy prickle across the back of her neck and glance up to see him watching, staring.

Did anyone know where I spent the night? Does Trevor?

"Sure, an' I heard it meself," a reed-thin man in worn overalls said as Molly served him a plate with breakfast. He turned to another worker behind him in the serving line, insistent on getting the other man to believe what he was saying.

Molly scooped eggs onto the tin plate and reached for the second man's plate.

"Aw, and why would the muckety-mucks do anythin' not right?" The second man asked with a suspicious twist to his chapped lips. "They make enough money, don't they? Why'd they go agin' the law?"

"You listen to me, John Barley," the first man stopped to shake his fork in the other man's face. "I only know what I heard from the gal works in the saloon. She said there's a plan to do something wrong an' a lot of them what's higher up knows about it."

"Like who?"

The talkative man motioned John Barley closer and spoke in a whisper. "Like Trevor Peterson for one, an' that engineer, Davis."

Half-listening to the conversation, Molly turned her full attention at the mention of Trevor's name. Although she wanted to stop the men and ask what they'd heard, a third man pushed his way forward.

"Gimme some of them eggs, Missy," he ordered, holding out a tin plate in a grubby, oil-stained hand. "Got to eat and git to work driving spikes."

The first two men moved away to sit at a table.

What was that all about? What's Trevor gotten himself into?

"Didja hear the whispers?" Clover asked after the breakfast rush as she lugged in a bushel basket of potatoes to peel for lunch.

"About what?" Molly asked. A wrinkle of worry creased her forehead. Even though she had no feelings for Trevor—not good ones anyway—she had heard a lot of troubling suspicions this morning. No one really knew what wrongdoing was being planned. Only that something was going on and it was illegal. Priscilla at the Commodore had witnessed a secret meeting and heard a few words of a plan.

The news had spread fast throughout the camp. Though no one really knew anything solid, just suppositions. What worried Molly most was that Priscilla had let slip Luke had been at the meeting.

Sure and would he be doin' something wrong with Trevor? She couldn't fit that notion with the man who'd asked so kindly to help her, nor with the battered survivor of that mysterious alley fight. *I'll not believe it.*

"Iris heard Mr. Peterson and some of his friends plan to cheat the UP somehow."

"How?"

Luke can't be considered one of those friends, can he?

Clover shrugged, sighed, and picked up a potato. "Not certain. News is just travelin' around."

"You best be mindin' your own affairs," Molly scolded as she picked up a potato and her paring knife. "Loose lips flappin' will cause you trouble, girl."

Although Clover's eyes narrowed with scorn, her lips soon took on a smirk. "Maybe so. An' maybe me and the rest of the girls were wonderin' why you didn't come back to the tent last night to sleep."

Anger boiled up in Molly, but she kept her eyes focused on the potato she was peeling. "Mind your own affairs," she repeated, knowing she hadn't heard the end of it.

***

Luke looked at the gun parts he'd crafted that morning, spread out on the worktable. All he needed to do now was assemble the small weapon for Molly. He'd decided to make the grip from mother of pearl—light and delicate like Molly. The gun would be small, but easy enough for her to handle.

She could hide it in a small reticule or even a pocket if necessary.

It could handle well and had enough power for Molly, with a kick that wouldn't knock her off her feet.

Once I teach her to shoot.

As he'd worked over the gun, Luke worried. He'd come in early that morning and begun work on the secret compartments he'd need to hide Trevor's crates. Although there was still a small amount of work to be done, Luke knew he could finish the job quickly.

Even though he had every intention of going along with Trevor's scheme, his heart was not in it.

I'm an honest man, not a thief!

The trouble was—Luke knew he'd have to find a way to inform Grenville Dodge about the scheme. To alert him that all was not as it seemed to be. It would mean explaining why he'd allowed himself to make a hidden compartment for Trevor's plans, but surely the man would understand.

Luke had never met Dodge in person, knowing only that he had been friends with General Grant during the war. The General spoke highly of Dodge, so he must be an honest man.

As he tightened the screws in the grips of Molly's gun, Luke thought of writing a letter. He could send it anonymously. But would it reach Dodge? Would he read it? Surely a man as busy as him would have people who read his mail, decided what was important or not. A letter without a signature might be seen as a prank or the ramblings of an unbalanced person.

I could write a note and give it to him secretly when he's here.

That way, he'd know I wrote it and I could somehow tell him it was an urgent matter.

But how?

Luke had no doubts that he would be watched closely by Trevor and his friends. They would want to make certain Luke planned to follow through.

I need to help stop this crime.

He'd wanted to discuss last night's meeting with Molly. But after that brief stint of gun practice, he and Molly had both gone to their respective beds.

Strange I'd feel a spark of....what...? with Molly. Not after I vowed never to love another woman after Betty.

Luke had lain awake most of the night, drifting off to sleep just before dawn. When he woke, Molly had already left for a long day in the cook tent. He knew from talking to Harry that the girls who did the cooking worked from long before dawn to long after dark.

I wish Greg were here. Maybe I can talk to Harry.

Shouting from outside the open-air shack drew Luke's attention. He laid Molly's gun down on the worktable and went out one of the side openings. Swarms of workers were tossing down chisels, picks, leaving overturned wheelbarrows and racing toward a runaway wagon. The wagon, pulled by lathered horses, clattered across the rough ground, finally coming to a stop beside a railroad car sitting on the track.

Workers swarmed over the side of the wagon. A woman screamed and started to weep.

"What's wrong? What's happened?" Luke questioned as Muchen ran past, his long dark braid flopping along his back.

Muchen raised his hands and spoke in rapid Chinese. He never stopped his forward motion toward the wagon.

Luke hurried after Muchen, arriving at the wagon just as someone pulled a limp body from the wagon bed. He didn't know everyone in camp, but Luke recognized the freed Black, Randal, who had done such an outstanding job at the drill site. A second body, drilled through the heart by a Sioux arrow, was O'Flynn.

"Sean!" A woman screamed and fell to her knees. Other women gathered around her, murmuring and comforting. Her anguished cries were muffled as she covered her face with a tattered calico apron.

"What happened?" Luke asked again, trying to get an answer from any of the grim-faced men standing around the wagon.

The group of Chinese, including Muchen, began to wail in anguish as a third body was pulled from the wagon. While Luke had tried to learn a few words of the unfamiliar language, he didn't need an interpreter to understand Muchen's agonized words. Grief was the same in any language.

The wagon's driver, an older man with a white beard and bloodshot eyes, trembled at the reins. He'd stopped the wagon, thrown on the brake, but sat frozen on the wagon seat staring off into the distance. After one startled glance, Luke noticed an arrow pierced through the man's battered brown hat.

A second crew of workers rode up more slowly on another wagon, their faces grim. As they climbed slowly out of the wagon, people rushed up, questioning, talking.

“What happened?” Luke asked again, having to yell over the loud weeping and murmurs of the crowd. More people hurried over from the Labor Camp, abandoning their jobs. An eerie silence took over where the usual clamoring of picks chiseling stone and the pounding of the metal ties beat at the ear. “How did these men die?”

“Sioux!” A man stalked up, his face dirt smudged and splashed with blood. He quivered with rage. “Look at the arrow. They’ve been fighting us all along for coming across their land. Why ain’t the UP protecting us from them savages?”

“It was an ambush,” a man in grimy coveralls spewed the words. He spit a chaw of well-chewed tobacco. “No sooner had Randal and O’Flynn got ready to pour in the blastin’ powder then we saw the arrows fly. Poor devils never had a chance.”

In the midst of everyone, Davis rode up on a brown and white spotted horse. “What’s going on here? Why are you men stopping work!”

Harry stepped up boldly. “Men have died, Mr. Davis. We’ll be takin’ time to pay respects.”

Davis sputtered, his face growing red. When he saw that two of the dead men were his top drilling team, he spewed out a string of curses. “Someone needs to stop those murderers. The UPR project can’t continue if they keep stopping us, wasting time because the railroad crosses their land. It’s that devil Red Cloud! He’s holding up progress.”

Men have died and all he thinks about is progress.

Luke clenched his hands and kept his mouth shut. He had plenty he’d like to say, but he also had a task to accomplish here.

What was it Mrs. O'Shay used to say? "Wise as a serpent, quiet as a dove."

I'll keep quiet until I know enough to strike back.

Chapter Eighteen

There was no more work that day. The bodies were carried to the undertaker in town, their mourning families trudging behind. An air of uneasy silence filled the town and the labor camp. People milled about in low-voiced groups, giving Luke uneasy glances as he strode into town. A somber mood covered the town like a gray blanket of fog.

Although usually noisy almost to the point of distraction, today the town had been silenced. There were no hammers pounding in spikes or driving the wooden ties in place. No shouts or calls for the water boy. The steady screech and hiss of the railroad cars traveling across the newly laid tracks was silent. Men's voices were subdued or mournful. There was no constant chatter of different languages, no clang as the iron rails were dropped into place.

Luke walked toward the saloon, too fidgety to work on railroad business or even Molly's gun. The deaths had jarred him. He knew the survivors' mourning well. Even though he hadn't known the men who died well, he had at least spoken to them.

Yesterday at this time, they had no idea it would be their last day on earth.

It was a sobering reminder to Luke that one of the bodies could easily have been his. Unless he worked Trevor's scheme, he could find himself in an early grave.

A group of men had gathered in the Commodore. Trevor stood between the mayor and a few of the leading citizens. As Luke walked through the swinging doors and headed to the bar, he could hear Trevor's loud voice, shouting orders.

"We can't wait for word from headquarters. We need to kill those savages and move on. They are stopping progress on the railroad. The Central Pacific is laying up to six miles of track a day. We aren't able to keep up because of those Indians."

Luke knew the battle between the UP and the CP had been heated all along. Rumors flew back and forth about each railroad's track laying progress. He'd heard the government and investors were paying up to $16,000 for every mile of track laid and 20 sections of land. It was enough of an incentive to lead many to unscrupulous ways to accomplish the goal.

"Each day we can't lay track, we lose money," Trevor groused. "We need those savages stopped."

"How do you propose we do that?" Mayor Willoughby asked. A short, balding man, he wiped sweat from his brow. "The UP has said we should try to get along with the local people, to displace them as little as possible."

Luke ordered a beer, more for something to do with his hands than to drink.

"And let them kill more of our workers?" Trevor shouted back. "Randal and O'Flynn were two of our best drillers. I say it's time we wipe them out."

Having heard all he wanted to hear, Luke turned from the bar, mug of beer in hand. "How will that help?"

Trevor turned his way with a murderous look. "Were you speaking, Morgan?"

Luke knew he was treading on thin ice, but he felt compelled to speak. "Killing the Indians isn't the wisest decision. Sure, you can kill the ones who murdered our crew, but there will be more. There're whole tribes out there where the railroad has to cross their land."

"Then we need to be free of them all!" Trevor insisted. "The railroad must come first. We need that land."

"No, that's not the way," Luke shook his head. "There's a better way."

Harry had been standing at the end of the bar. Now he walked forward so that he stood beside Luke. "What's your idea, lad?"

"The UP is going to be going across a lot of country out there," Luke looked around at the group of men, some workers, some officials, filling the smoke-filled room. "We're going to be traveling this route many times. Wouldn't it be wiser to make peace with the tribes instead of killing them off a few at a time?"

"Peace," Trevor spoke the word as if it left a nasty taste in his mouth. "Just what do you think we've been trying to do in the last six months before you got here? The Indians lie and agree, then go behind our backs. They aren't willing to aim for peace. They pull out our surveying stakes and toss them on a fire. We've lost crucial time and money trying to deal with them."

"Hear the lad out," Harry insisted. "I've not seen your way movin' us forward, Mr. Peterson. Or findin' any solutions'."

"If we kill this tribe, then innocent travelers who ride the railroad later, may die. The Indians will consider we are at war with them. We took their land and gave them nothing in return. Then we killed some of them to move forward. Many of those tribes are probably just defending their home, just like many of us would. The UP came roaring in with the "iron horse" and took it over. We need to find a way to work in agreement with them."

Some of the workers in the crowd murmured and nodded. Harry gave a slow nod in agreement. "Makes sense to me. Peace now and safe passage for others. Seems to me a better way to get along."

Trevor dismissed the idea, his face twisted with anger. He tried to shout over the crowd, but people had begun to voice their own opinions. Davis tried to encourage people to agree with Trevor, but more and more people sided with Luke.

Voices raised, men argued, and the room quickly surged with emotion. Fueled no doubt by the realization the Indians could fire and kill any one of them too.

"All right, then," Davis roared out over the crowd, "if we don't use violence to subdue these savages. What do you have in mind?"

Harry agreed, running a hand over his whiskered chin, "That so, lad, what is it you have in mind? You have a plan, without gettin' yourself killed too?"

After taking a quick swallow of beer, Luke looked around at all the faces staring at him. Although he'd often been a leader in his community in New York, he didn't like to presume only his ideas mattered. Still, anything to prevent more violence had to be worth an attempt. Someone had to give a gesture of peace before things grew out of control. "I think so."

***

"Sure an' I hope this works," Molly said as she walked behind the wagon, holding a lead rope on a cow. Bawling its disapproval, a brown and white calf followed close behind. A couple of lambs being led in the hands of Chinese workers bleated uncertainly. A crate of chickens in the wagon bed squawked, annoyed at being penned.

It had been Luke's idea to present Chief Red Cloud and his tribe with livestock and supplies. Gifts to sweeten the request he hoped to make to the tribal leader. As he drove the wagon toward the section of track where the men had been killed, Luke said a quick prayer.

Let this work.

Walking alongside the wagon, Muchen, his hands tucked inside the wide sleeves of his red silk tunic, spoke, "Give gifts. Make friend."

Two other Irishmen, friends of Harry, were the only ones Luke had persuaded to join him on what might be a fool's errand. One chubby, bearded man with a head of flaming red hair rode a plodding mule and led two other pack mules loaded with saddlebags bulging with gifts for the Sioux—blankets, bolts of cloth, salves, and dozens of other necessary items the Indians traded for regularly at the Indian Trading Post.

In the wagon, Luke had loaded sacks of potatoes, onions, apples, carrots, a few sides of beef and various other foodstuffs. Enough to give the starving tribe a boost through the coming winter.

I sure hope this works. Harry and Julie thought it would.

After Luke's statement in the Commodore, that he wanted to attempt peace with the tribes, Harry had led him home to supper. "Come'n have a meal with us," Harry urged, "I can tell you what you'll be needin' to know about Chief Red Cloud."

"The UP's already havin' a time with him. He's verra protective of his tribe and his land," Harry explained as they sat around his plank table, eating by lamplight.

“At first,” Julie said, placing a plate of Irish stew before Luke at the dinner table, “the UP got along fine with the Chief. They were polite and respectful, told him where they’d be working and even helped him move the village once. Then Trevor showed up and he ran roughshod over them. Acted like they were no more’n bugs to be squashed.”

Digging into his stew, Harry agreed with his wife. “It’s been a beastly business all around. I don’t think Chief Red Cloud would have killed anyone if we’d been honest and kept our word.”

“Ha!” Julie muttered, going to pick up little Bonnie. “Honest is not a word you’d be usin’ for Trevor Peterson.”

Holding steady to the reins of the harness, Luke cringed in memory. He’d wanted to tell Harry and Julie about his plan to “help” Trevor with his scheme. To explain why he needed to skirt the law for a time. Just until he could get enough information to prove Greg’s death was murder. There hadn’t been a second during the meal. Afterwards, Luke hurried back to his cabin to make plans for a visit to Red Cloud.

What will Harry and Julie think of me when they know? Will they understand?

“Looks like we been spotted,” Patrick, the redhead, whispered from his seat on the mule’s bare back.

Chapter Nineteen

Luke pulled the wagon to a halt. On a small rise – near where the murdered men had been drilling into a mountain of rock—three Sioux warriors sat silent and proud on bareback horses.

"That's Chief Red Cloud wearin' the buckskin with fringed sleeves," Patrick told Luke.

Red Cloud's long dark hair flowed freely across his shoulders. Dark eyes studied them with an unreadable expression. His ancient, lined face had weathered brown as leather from the sun.

"He speaks English well," the second Irishman, Clyve, spoke up. "Enough to know when the likes of Trevor Peterson lies to him."

"Let me approach him," Luke pulled back on the wagon's reins. He set the brake.

One of the lambs bleated and Molly shushed him. "Go with God," she murmured.

Luke climbed from the wagon. Holding up his hands in peace, he walked slowly toward the chief.

Red Cloud rode down the mountain, the glossy tan stallion picking his way over the rocks.

"Chief," Luke began, "My name is Luke Morgan."

"You work iron horse?"

"Yes, sir, in a way. I'm a blacksmith." He left out the part about being a gunsmith too. Surely, from what Luke read, Red Cloud had endured enough from the white man's guns.

Red Cloud sat silent and proud. Back straight. Expression inscrutable. Waiting.

Luke motioned toward the men who had followed him. Muchen. Patrick O'Flynn, Clyve, a couple of the freed Blacks who had worked laying track. Molly, who had insisted on coming along to keep the animals calm. Although a lot of the men had agreed Luke had a good plan, Trevor had insisted most go back to work today. When the workers balked at Luke's plan being dismissed, Trevor gave reluctant permission for a few people to join him.

"You'll not lose a day's pay if you follow Morgan," Trevor had agreed, "if you come back alive."

"It may work," Mayor Willoughby had said, although the fear in his eyes showed his doubts.

"We come to offer peace," Luke said. "We bring gifts."

"Hah!" The proud man spit on the ground, as if dismissing any idea of a white man's peace. "You take. Lie. Make promises and break."

"I can't deny that. You have suffered great losses. But so have we." He pointed at Patrick. "His brother was killed the other day, just doing his job. This man–" He pointed next at Muchen. "His people face many hardships to come to this country to work, be free. Not all of us agree with the tactics—the plans—of the railroad. Not all of us lie and break treaties. We too face hardships."

Red Cloud's face seemed to soften as he noticed Molly behind the wagon, holding tight to the rope around the cow's neck.

"We come in peace to ask you to consider working with us. We know you have been displaced," Luke made a motion with his hands to signify what the word meant, "and we want to help you. We have brought gifts, animals..."

"Why?"

"If you will allow the iron horse to move forward, we will give you supplies—food, animals, cloth, whatever you have need of. We will pay for the use of your land."

"One time?" Red Cloud asked, suspicion in his eyes. "When you come many times? Destroy our hunting ground? Kill our buffalo? We fill our children's bellies once and starve after?"

Luke shook his head. "No. Many times." He thought hard about how to explain a yearly barter through the few words they could share. "Each harvest time, we bring more. Each time, you allow the train to move freely across your land."

"How will we know where the iron horse travels? What land he will use?"

"I can show you on a survey map," Luke said, although unsure how much the chief would understand of a white man's map. "The wooden stakes we place in the ground show the progress of the tracks. If you have a disagreement, or can think of a better way, we will talk."

Red Cloud grimaced as if he didn't find this the best solution. It took Luke a few more minutes of explanation before Red Cloud showed signs he understood.

"This is satisfactory," the chief spoke, surprising Luke with his command of the English language. But then, hadn't Harry said the chief often had dealings with the government about treaties?

I suppose he had to learn to defend his people.

The chief motioned to the other braves sitting on the hill. They rode forward to accept the gifts. Patrick handed over the mules and the bulging saddle bags. Kind-hearted Molly shed a tear or two as they took the lambs and chickens, the cow and small calf.

“We let your men from the iron horse move to the sticks in the ground,” Red Cloud pointed to the survey sticks. “If you break this promise, we kill again.”

“We will not break this promise,” Luke said, determined somehow to get Grenville Dodge or an official of the UP to make certain of that. Anyone but Trevor Peterson or his men.

On the way home, sitting beside him on the wagon seat, Molly said, “Well, an’ you’ll be returnin’ a hero. You made an agreement with the tribe to let the UP be crossin’ their land.”

“Hardly,” Luke answered, even though he felt good about what he’d accomplished that day. “Several good men had to die before Red Cloud was given what he wanted. I wish Trevor had used more compassion to talk to them before that happened.”

“Buildin’ a railroad’s dangerous business,” Molly said. “Built on the backs and the graves of many a man.”

Holding the reins loosely in his hands, Luke nodded. Although his legs still trembled from the strain of standing up to Red Cloud, he felt good. Warm and comforted as if he’d been an instrument of peace. Like Betty often said when he helped solve a conflict in his community, “You made a difference, Luke. That counts for something.”

It had been Molly’s idea to take along the cow and calf so the children could have fresh milk. Like Molly today, Betty would have been right there making sure the Indian children were given food and warm clothing. For the first time in a long time, Luke smiled when he thought of his departed wife. A smile quickly replaced by a grim clenching of his teeth as Patrick shouted from behind the wagon.

"Fire!"

Chapter Twenty

"Fire!" Patrick shouted again, standing up in the stirrups and craning his neck to see.

Luke glanced up, shocked to see massive clouds of rolling gray smoke rising over where the town and Labor Camp should be.

Fire!

"The camp!" Molly shouted, "it's on fire!"

Luke slapped the reins down on the backs of the horses and sent them and the wagon cantering toward the center of town. The other men on mules galloped past, intent on getting to the scene of the disaster. Beside him on the wagon seat, Molly clung to the edge and held on tight. The wagon wheels clattered over the uneven ground, hitting rocks that jarred them up and down.

One jolt caused Luke to bite his tongue. He tasted blood but kept slapping the reins, urging the horses forward.

Some of the buildings in town were burning, although few seemed to be engulfed in fire. The same couldn't be said of the one settlement of shacks where many of the UP workers lived with their families. Even as Luke jumped from the wagon, he could see the billows of smoke rising from the canvas tents. Women and children either running around dazed, or screaming in fear. Other workers—a mix of Chinese, Irish, freed Blacks and whites—ran here and there trying to put out the flames.

The scene was one of chaos, the streets teeming with people and animals. Luke hurried to join a bucket brigade, trying to save two of the worker's shacks. The chaos turned into teamwork. Other workers ran up, tossing buckets on the flames, helping women and children to safety. Most of the worker's settlement, including the mess tent, appeared to be ruins.

What happened? It must have been a stray spark. A cookstove left untended. An accident. Surely. What other explanation could there be?

Luke sloshed water on a burning wall of canvas, a suspicion gnawing in the pit of his stomach. The fires were vicious, but scattered. If they'd started by accident, wouldn't they have spread out from a single starting point?

He looked up at a scraping footstep to see Julie, holding baby Bonnie, walking by in a daze. A shattered look on her face, her red calico ripped and dragging. With each step she almost tripped over the torn fabric. Oddly enough, she wore no shoes.

"Julie? Where's Harry? What happened?" Luke asked.

She looked at him as if she didn't know who he was. Baby Bonnie stared at him with her solemn green eyes, a tiny smile quirking at her lips. Soot smudged the baby's face but otherwise she looked unharmed. Julie had a scratch across her forehead oozing blood.

"Julie?"

When he spoke her name again, she finally looked at him. "Luke?"

"What happened here? Who did this?"

Molly ran toward Julie, holding out a dipper of water. "Here, take a drink. Tell us what happened."

Julie drank gratefully but unseeingly, her eyes fixed on Luke. She shifted the baby in her arms. "Harry? Harry's dead."

The news slammed Luke like a sledgehammer. “Dead? How?”

The woman shook her head, still dazed. “Fire broke out in the worker’s camp. He was tryin’ to get some of the children out of a building. He ran back in and tossed a little boy out the window. Before he could get out, the roof caved in on him.”

“Maybe he’s just hurt, where is he?” Luke made a movement to rush to his friend’s aid.

Julie waved her hand to the charred and smoldering ruins of a small building. “Gone, gone. Harry’s gone.” As if suddenly aware of her words, Julie began to weep and dropped to the muddy ground. If Molly hadn’t grabbed Bonnie, the baby would have slid from her mother’s arms.

“We need help over here,” someone called. “We can save these homes.”

Luke turned toward the men, torn between helping Julie and fighting the fire. A group of Chinese surged past, carrying buckets, dripping water in the streets. The dusty road had turned quickly to mud and squelched into oozing puddles. People ran by spattering mud and slipping in the treacherous muck.

“I’ll find a safe place for her,” Molly said as if she understood Luke’s dilemma. “An’ the babe.”

“All right but come back here when you’ve done that. We don’t know where Trevor is in all this. You shouldn’t be alone to deal with him.”

Where’s Trevor? Or Davis? Why weren’t they here protecting the UP’s property?

Strange, Luke thought as he looked around at the crowds of people fighting the flames. He saw none of the officials – Trevor, Davis and even Mayor Willoughby were strangely absent.

"Julie, do you know how this started? Was it an accident?"

Almost in a daze again, Julie looked around at the flames, the billows of dark smoke. Cinders filled the air and people rushed around splashing water on any spark or flame. Julie stared with unseeing eyes.

"Tis unaware she is," Molly chided Luke. "I'll take her to the other girls, they'll care for her."

Molly led Julie away and Luke turned back to fighting the fire.

"Here, let's get more buckets going," he shouted to Muchen and his men. "Maybe we can save the hotel."

The Chinese were quick to follow his lead, tossing buckets of water on the smoldering flames. They'd managed to squelch a small fire eating away at the hotel's wraparound porch and moved on to extinguish another small fire on the steps.

Strange how those fires seemed planned. Contained. Luke walked into the alley between the hotel and telegraph office. A pile of smoldering boxes sent out puffs of smoke. Luke leaned down for a closer look, his eyes narrowing. Odd. The boxes were sitting exactly in the middle of the alley, as if started on purpose. They weren't even close to a building. Nowhere a stray spark could have drifted.

Why?

Who would have started fires and caused this destruction?

Luke couldn't understand. Had Red Cloud's men reneged already on the treaty? *Before we got back? He'd have had to send some of the tribe while we were talking peace. Why would he?*

Who else would want to stop the building of the UP? This would put a wrench in Trevor's progress. Luke could see piles of railroad lumber burning like the biggest bonfire ever near one edge of the camp.

Surely not anyone working on the project. Unless in retaliation for their family getting killed. But that didn't make sense either. The Chinese and Irish had very little in the way of possessions. Why would they burn their own homes?

Most of the town buildings had containable fires. The worker's shacks and tents had not been so fortunate. Smoke and ash rained down and burnt Luke's eyes. They watered and made everything blur. He choked on the smoke.

As he stepped into the alley, Luke felt a hand grab the back of his hair. Another hand snaked around his neck and jerked him back against a hefty body in a clench hold.

"What are you..."

The man yanked a burlap sack over Luke's head and dragged him further back into the alley's shadows. "Listen Morgan, if you know what's good for you, you'll keep your nose out of our business and away from Molly!"

Luke struggled to free himself from the man's strong arms. That same scent of bay rum and cigars beat against his nose. *Was it Trevor's men who had started the fire? Why? For what purpose? To ruin their own supplies? It made no sense.*

I agreed to do their dirty work on the railroad car. Why attack me now?

"Hey!" Muchen yelled in English and then a rapid spattering of Chinese. The unknown man holding Luke let him go. But not before a second man punched Luke in the stomach.

Luke struggled to tug off the burlap sack, but he didn't see the men who scurried into the shadows.

"Did you see them?" he questioned Muchen. "Do you know who they are?"

Muchen shook his head. "Bad men."

A gunshot drew their attention to the street. Luke glanced up to see Molly running through the muck, a look of terror on her face.

Behind her, Trevor chased on the bay. A couple of other rough-looking men Luke didn't know tried to cut off Molly's escape. Trevor's men probably. They chuckled and hollered, delighted in Molly's frightened face and stumbling flight. At every second, Molly's long skirt threatened to trip her and plunk her face down in the mud. Her long red hair streamed behind, the curls loosened by her frantic pace.

"Molly! Here!" Luke shouted.

Molly darted into the alley and Luke grabbed her by the hand. As if aware of the situation, Muchen darted in front of the horses and began to gibber in excited Chinese. One of the horses whinnied and shied, rising to his back legs. The horse's front legs pawed the air as Muchen darted out of its deadly path.

It gave Luke and Molly the start they needed to dash down the alley and behind the hotel. Behind them, they could hear the men shouting, enraged at Muchen. Luke could only hope the man got away.

"What's happen' here?" Molly gasped as Luke led her behind one building after another. "Has the world gone mad?"

"I don't know," Luke panted as they darted around people still fighting the fires, trying to avoid anyone on horseback. Down alleys and out on the other side of the street, Luke held tight to Molly's warm hand. One of the rough men, a jagged scar on his right cheek, followed them with evil intent. Each time Luke thought they'd lost him, the man showed up on his giant black quarter horse, grinning like a snake. He cut them off several times, but Luke managed to half grab, half drag Molly up stairs and across the boardwalk. They darted behind buildings and down alleys, looking over their shoulders.

At one point, hiding behind a stack of crates outside the Commodore, Luke thought for sure they were caught. At the last second, the rider turned and went in another direction away from their hiding place.

Molly opened her mouth to speak, but Luke put a cautious hand over her lips. Shook his head slightly. Panting himself, he worked to control his ragged breath, to keep quiet.

"They aren't here," a gruff voice hollered close by, "they musta' got away."

"Let's go," Trevor said from a short distance, "we've got business tonight. Just make sure they don't follow. We'll deal with the problem later."

What problem? Me? Molly?

Luke leaned against the slatted boards of the saloon and breathed deeply. His lungs filled with smoke-tinged air. Beside him, Molly leaned forward, hands on knees, and gasped for breath. Her mottled face flamed splotches of red from their mad dash through the streets.

Luke and Molly stayed hidden a while longer. "I need to follow Trevor and see what's going on," Luke whispered after making sure no one was around. "None of this makes sense."

"If your goin', I'm goin' along."

"Now, Molly, you need to go back to the cabin and stay safe," Luke said, although he had doubts about her safety anywhere. None of this evening made sense. The fires, the threat in the alley. The chase.

Although the air still filled with the pungent odor of smoke and people rushed around, the fire seemed to be under control.

What is going on around here? Maybe Molly's right and the world has gone mad?

"Safe?" She stiffened her body and jerked away from him, "sure an' what place is that when the town was set on fire? If Trevor finds me, sure an' I'm not safe anywhere."

In the twilight, Luke could see those green eyes blazing at him, little glints of anger shooting sparks. Her lips stitched in a tight line. Molly's tiny body stood up straight and tall. Determined, if the fists pressed to the hips of her green checked dress were any indication.

He had to agree, keeping Molly with him seemed the safest choice. Luke had no doubt if he refused to take her, Molly would find a way to trail along anyway.

"All right," he agreed reluctantly, with a flickering smile at her courage. "But we need to stay calm and not go dashing off like a jackrabbit. You need to follow my lead and do what I say. Agreed?"

Molly grumbled but nodded.

Again, he took her hand, surprised at the warmth and the way it fit snugly within his own. “Let’s go.”

Chapter Twenty-One

Molly didn't know how long they walked after they left the smoldering town. Or even how Luke knew which way to go. He had started off toward the woods at the edge of town. Away from where the railroad tracks led off across the prairie. Almost down near where the big river ran deep and wide. Molly and the other cooking girls had walked down there once. Before their duties slaving to cook meals had taken over their lives. Short walks to the privy were their only private moments now.

The sliver of a moon came out and played hide and seek with the clouds. The world glowed bright at times, then the shadows deepened as Molly followed Luke cautiously. Luke kept them in the shadows under the tree line. More than once, he motioned Molly to stop and crouch behind a bunch of bushes as they heard a noise.

Dashin' off like a jackrabbit!

As she trudged along the uneven road, Molly fumed. They hadn't taken more than a few steps outside of town when she pulled her hand out of Luke's. Angered, although she couldn't understand why.

Like I'm a wee sprite he has to scold.

No one could be more afraid of Trevor than me, Molly thought. *Whatever the man's into, it's evil business for sure. Whatever he's hidin' in the woods has no good behind it.*

The beginnings of a headache prickled behind her eyes. Molly took deep breaths of the night-scented air. They'd left the smoky, charred scent of the town and camp behind. As she walked, Molly cleared her raspy throat of the harsh, wood ash smell. The refreshing scent of pines and a faint summer breeze made the walk almost pleasant. Molly could have enjoyed the night, except for the frightened pounding of her heart and the quivering of her limbs.

What if we run into Trevor out here?

Molly still feared Trevor's anger about her smacking him with the skillet. He could be brutal. What if he were out here lyin' in wait? A shudder went through her body. Warm tears dripped out of her eyes.

Oh, Ma an' Da, why did I ever leave Ireland?

"Quiet, now," Luke whispered almost in her ear. "I think there's something in the woods."

Frightened, Molly clutched Luke's linen shirt sleeve and followed cautiously. Until he tugged her free and motioned her to hide behind a fresh-scented pine.

"Wait here. Let me go see what's happening."

"No."

As gently as if she were a child, he unfolded her fingers from his shirt. "It will be all right, Molly. You wait here while I go see what's going on. If I don't come back, you can run for help."

Molly trembled but loosened her fingers from his shirt. Her lips moved but she couldn't get a prayer past them. Instead, she prayed silently in her heart for Luke's safe return.

The moon chose that second to slip behind a cloud, leaving the world in shadowy darkness. From her hiding place behind a tree, Molly could see dark shapes and slightly lighter splotches. Time wore on, and her eyes strained as she clung to a pine trunk and focused on where she'd last seen Luke moving cautiously toward the woods.

Suddenly, a dark shape rushed toward Molly's hiding place. She opened her mouth to scream when a hand clamped it shut. Molly raised her leg to bring her heel down on top of the person's foot.

"Shush, shush, it's me, Luke."

Caught off balance trying to stomp his boot, Molly fell into his arms. His hand eased off her mouth. "Hush, now," he cautioned, "I didn't see any guards around, but we can't be too careful."

"What is it?"

"I found a wagon full of women," Luke's breath sounded ragged, "like a prison wagon. I couldn't get close enough to talk to them, but I'm pretty sure I recognized Priscilla from the saloon."

Molly gasped.

"Sure an' why would a wagon full of women be out here in the woods?"

"I'm not sure," Luke said. "I could see a stout lock on the outside. If I was sure no one was guarding the wagon, I could probably break the lock with a rock. But, breaking anything with a rock is a loud business. No sense announcing we're out here."

"Well let's be goin' then!" Molly started to dash away from the hiding place.

Luke caught her arm and held tight. "Not so fast. We don't know what's going on here. Trevor or any of his men could be sitting somewhere waiting, watching. If we get caught too, we are no help to the women."

"What can we do?"

"Let me think," Luke said as he peered into the darkening woods. "We need to be patient."

Molly fumed. She wanted to pace up and down, but fear kept her frozen in place.

They waited a while to see if anyone would come back to the wagon. At one point, they did hear a couple of riders approach. The women inside the wagon grew excited and cried out in fear and anger. They fell quiet at harsh voices screaming for them to be silent. The men spoke but Molly and Luke were too far away to hear anything. After another half hour or so, the riders left. The women in the wagon yelled and called out. Their voices blended with the chirping of crickets and the sleepy calls of night birds. Far off in the distance, a lonely wolf howled his discomfort.

One by one the voices in the wagon grew silent. The moon faded and left an eerie blue gray shadow over the world.

"Molly, I think the best thing to do is for me to go get something to pick the lock or break it," Luke finally decided. "Do you think you can wait here? If the wagon moves out, you can let me know where it goes. I shouldn't be gone long. I probably need a gun too."

The idea terrified her, but Molly had been thinking all the while Luke had. She had a couple of ideas of her own. Plans Luke would certainly not approve of.

Jackrabbit indeed!

"Sure an' you just hurry back," Molly said, surprised at the trembling in her voice.

"Keep hidden and stay out of sight," Luke cautioned as he turned to go back toward the smoldering town. "I'll return as soon as I can. It shouldn't take long."

"I'll be goin' to find out what's goin' on," Molly stated to herself a few minutes after Luke's shadow had eased away into the darkness. "We canna leave those women out there all night. Not for Trevor's plans—whatever those might be."

Molly tugged down the bodice of her green dress as if preparing for a social call. Swallowed hard to get up her courage. "I'll be goin'. If they're all women in there, maybe they'll talk to me."

"You'll get caught."

That's what Luke would be sayin' if he knew what I planned to do.

Molly had no intention of getting caught. One of those voices had sounded suspiciously like Trevor. "I'll be comin' back," she promised, but only the rough bark of the pine tree heard the whisper.

Molly took her time in making a circuitous way to the wagon. The wagon—a huge, hulking wooden shape—sat beneath a covering of pine trees. It looked almost like a circus wagon she'd seen once—a big square box with a roof of wooden shingles. There were only a few windows high on the walls covered with iron bars. It sure enough did look like a prison wagon. As Molly approached, a pale face appeared at one of the windows.

"Be careful," a voice whispered, "there might be a guard in the woods."

"Who are you?" Molly whispered back.

"Priscilla, from the Commodore."

An' how did Luke recognize her so fast?

Molly pursed her lips. *An' sure an' why do I care what the man does?*

"Why are you out here?"

A strangled sob came from the girl. "They're selling us! Down the road to one of those 'hell on wheels' towns. Just like the others. Aura Lee tried to tell me something was goin' on, but I didn't pay no mind."

Selling!

Molly's mind reeled. She'd heard of such things from the girls in camp. Stories of men who bought women and did terrible things with them. *Was that why Trevor had to be gone so much? Was this one of the things he called "side business?" The buyin' and sellin' of women?* Iris had often blathered out stories about places called "Hell on Wheels" where vile doings went on. They were make-shift railroad towns, built to satisfy the wrongful appetites of men. Whiskey, gambling and soiled women. Every time the railroad tracks eased a few more miles across the prairie, evil men would set up their tents and put out their offerings. Often, Iris had said, at outlandish prices.

"I'll get you out."

"You can't. We've tried," Priscilla moaned. "There is no way."

"Can you go for help?" another voice asked. A tear-smudged face appeared at the bars.

Julie! How did she get here? I left her safe with Iris and Clover.

Throwing caution to the wind, Molly eased her way around to the front of the wagon. A heavy door with a barred window did indeed have a stout lock. Thinking she might be able to break it, Molly searched around and found a rock.

I'm not as strong as Luke but maybe if I can hit it right...

A gasp from the window alerted Molly just before hands closed around her waist. As tight as a steel trap.

"Well, who do we have here," Trevor's voice said, his foul breath blowing across the back of Molly's neck. "Where is your beau? Not out here to protect you?"

"An' what are you doin' out here, Trevor?" Molly snapped, trying to twist out of his arms. She might be frightened out of her wits, but Molly knew enough not to show it. Trevor seemed to take delight in her fear.

Surely Luke will see what's happenin' when he comes back.

"Just a little business, Molly, sweet. It's too bad you had to put your nosy little self out here too."

Molly jerked and pulled but Trevor refused to let her go.

"Get back, all of you," he ordered the women in the wagon. "Now!"

A shuffling came from inside as the women backed away from the door.

Molly struggled, but he twisted her around to face the wagon's door. A small wooden step led up to it. Taking a key from his trouser pocket, Trevor unlocked the shiny lock and pulled it out of the hasp.

Inside the wagon, a baby's wail pierced the night.

Not little Bonnie!

With a shove, Trevor forced Molly up the step to the wagon's door. "Go get that baby. We're leaving here in the morning. I'm certain the saloon owner who wants this batch won't want a squalling baby along too."

"An' what am I to do with her then?" Molly questioned, trying to sound brave but knowing her shaky words gave away her fear.

"Leave her on the ground for all I care." Trevor dismissed the baby like a piece of rubbish. "We've no need of a baby."

What about me?

"Oh, please," Julie cried out, begging as she clutched Bonnie in her arms. The baby's frightened cries grew louder. Her tiny fists clutched the front of Julie's dress. "Have mercy. I can take her with me. She won't stop me from anything I'm made to do. I can work with her along. I beg you, please. Please."

"Shut up!" Trevor snapped. "Get the baby, Molly."

He shoved her into the midst of about eight women. Molly struggled to get her footing. The wagon's uneven plank flooring made standing a treacherous ordeal. Turning to face him, she snapped, "An' what if I won't?"

Thoughts raced through her mind. Was it better to rescue Bonnie and leave her in the woods, knowing Luke would find her? Or better to let Julie fight her own battle?

"Please," Julie cried again, "I've lost my husband. Don't take my baby too."

Trevor threw up his hands in disgust. He sneered as he looked around at Julie. "Fine! Keep the brat. Let your new owner deal with you and her. And don't come crying if he decides to drown her."

Before Molly could quite understand what was happening, Trevor jumped off the wagon's step, slammed the heavy door and clasped the lock. Molly's heart plunged to the tips of her high button shoes when she heard the key turn and the lock snap tight.

"There you go, my sweet," Trevor's face peered at her through the bars. "You know, Molly, my love, I did love you. So unspoiled, so pure and even if you were of a lower race, I thought to make something tolerable of you. But, perhaps, you'll bring a higher price to some other man. Goodbye, my love."

One of the women sobbed. Baby Bonnie whimpered. Another woman prayed in a mutter of a foreign language.

Now, I'm a prisoner too!

Chapter Twenty-Two

It was the longest night Luke had ever endured. Even longer than the one, gut-wrenching night he'd spent in his murdered family's home, weeping in a house that had known so much joy. The minutes dragged by like days. Tonight, staring at the dark blotch of the wagon, Luke felt as if time stood still.

Again.

He'd run as fast as he could to find some type of tool to break the lock. As if God were on his side, Luke had stumbled into a work area about half a mile from the woods. He'd found a hammer, a chisel and even a canteen full of sluggish, warm water. It quenched his bone-dry thirst after running and lightened his heart for a second.

God does care.

Guilt ate away at his insides once he returned to where he'd left Molly hiding. *Why did I leave her?*

Alone in the hiding place, Luke became aware that whispered voices were coming from near the wagon. It only took seconds for him to realize a conversation from the wagon included Molly's voice.

Molly! Why didn't you wait here like I told you?

Standing off to the side, Luke heard the conversation between Molly and Priscilla. His stomach lurched at the idea of Trevor selling women to saloon owners in other towns. *What a vile thing!*

Luke knew from reading the newspapers that towns grew like toadstools as they followed the building of the railroad. Many of those towns mushroomed overnight, having tent saloons, bawdy houses, and brothels to supply the "needs" of a variety of tastes. One town gave home to over one hundred saloons! Women were brought in to supply the "customers". The war had ended slavery for one group of people, but there was always someone who wanted to enslave someone else.

Trafficking women was a sickening, despicable practice. But the law abiding were few and far between out in this country. Even in towns with a sheriff, or within distance of a federal marshal, men could hide their sinful habits. Rarely did a woman escape or survive after being taken captive. Luke knew that General Casement, one of the superintendents of the UP, had cleared out one such town, Julesburg, by filling a graveyard. Rightly or wrongly, he had silenced a rowdy crowd that had led to the deaths of several UP workers in fights over gambling or drinking. Was it murder or justice? Luke had been unable to decide.

One afternoon, Harry had told him about men who traded some of the young, Chinese girls as slaves. It turned Luke's stomach, imagining his own sweet little Hannah in such a predicament. Now, it looked as if Molly and Priscilla were victims of the same type of men.

After Trevor locked Molly in with the others, several other men had come out of the woods.

I'm glad I didn't try to bust the lock earlier.

While his first instinct was to take the hammer, bash in the lock and free the women, Luke didn't dare.

If I'm captured, I'm no help to any of them.

"Keep a close watch on this bunch," Trevor ordered a man with a scarred face. "We'll pull out in the morning. I guess I'll have to show myself in town."

Another man laughed. “I guess those fires we started kept folks guessing so we could get a batch more women.”

Luke clenched his hands into fists, wanting to rush the men and pummel them into the ground. Only by sheer determination did he grit his teeth and keep his feet firmly planted. How dare they set fire to the camp just to capture more women!

“You idiot!” Trevor shouted. “I told you to start small fires, not burn down the whole Labor Camp. Those tents went up like fourth of July firecrackers! You were just supposed to use the fires as a distraction. You’ve ruined a lot of UP equipment that I’ll have to explain.”

The man spoke in a wheedling voice, “We tried, Mr. Peterson. Guess the wind got behind us and sent a spark into those tents. The things was covered with paraffin an’ went up like a wildfire.”

“No one was supposed to be killed either,” Trevor raged, “but one of my best construction men died. How will I replace Harry?”

“Now that wasn’t our fault!” A man argued back.

The dimness of the night kept Luke from pinpointing the voice.

“He jumped into a burning building. Who does that?”

Harry. Harry would.

“Even so,” Trevor argued back, “There have been enough accidents among the Irish. You need to use a better form of persuasion to get them to go along with our plans. We need them to help complete the railroad construction.”

Hiding nearby, Luke had no idea what most of Trevor’s confusing conversation meant. All he knew was that Trevor planned to take a wagon load of women and sell them in the morning. A wagon that included Molly, Julie, and baby Bonnie.

I won't let that happen, Harry.

How he planned to prevent the tragedy, Luke didn't know.

Trevor mounted his horse and headed back to town. Luke was careful to stay out of sight when the man passed. Although his first inclination was to rush the other men and free the women, Luke knew he couldn't. There were three men guarding the wagon. One began to build a campfire in the clearing near the wagon's door.

They'd kill him before he could get within a foot of the door, Luke knew. The idea pained him, but he had to stay free to help the women.

How?

It had to be after midnight. Luke had no idea what to do or where to go for help. Around Council Bluffs, Trevor's word was law. He had the mayor and no telling who else on his payroll. If Luke went to any of them, chances were he'd be caught and killed.

Who will rescue the women if I'm dead?

Luke knew he'd have to leave the women alone for the night. There was no other way. They should be safe in the wagon until he could get help. According to Trevor, the plan was to take them wherever they were going in the morning. They might be uncomfortable and frightened, but as merchandise they should not be harmed.

As fast as he dared, Luke made his way back to town. The fires had been extinguished but near the Labor Camps, a lot of people were crouched over campfires and makeshift shanties. Unsure where to go or who to ask for help, Luke heard his name called.

"Mr. Morgan, sir?" A young boy came out of the darkness, his face smudged, and one hand wrapped in a white bandage. "Me ma says to invite you to our campfire."

"Timmy?" Luke looked into the sad faces of a group sitting around a campfire. Behind them, the remains of their shanty still smoldered. A single battered tin cup sat on top of the fire. "Is that you?"

"Yes, sir, 'tis me family."

Luke walked toward the group and sat wearily on a log.

Mr. Burns—Timmy's da, he'd learned—was a spike driver. "'Tis pleased I am you be unharmed." Mr. Burns' Irish lilt fell flat with dejection. "Yer friend, Harry, he be the one who saved me Tim's life."

Mrs. Burns dabbed at her red rimmed eyes with a torn apron, "A fine man, fine. Tossed Tim out of the flames he did. We tried to pull him out but couldna."

A lump formed in Luke's throat, and he couldn't speak. His mind ached with the knowledge about Molly and the other women. Questions darted like arrows into his brain.

What will I do? How can I help them?

"Mum," a little girl whimpered, "I'm hungry."

Luke shook off his own troubles to look around at the sorry circle of the Burns' family. Even though it must have been after midnight, he suddenly realized the family had nowhere to go. "Do you not have food?"

"No, the fire..." Mrs. Burns started to speak but her husband cut her off.

"Mr. Peterson will help us out in the mornin'," Mr. Burns spoke up, authority in his words. He glared at the whimpering little girl. "Shush your grumbles."

The woman muttered a curse under her breath.

Luke sat up, pushing his own misery aside. Angered all over again about Trevor's men starting the fires, he couldn't decide whether to tell the Burn's the truth or not. In the end, he spoke up. "Trevor's the one who caused this misery, including Harry's death. He started the fire so his men could steal women from the camps." Even though the children stared, eyes as big as silver dollars, Luke plunged ahead. "You'll not get help from him."

The woman cried out.

"You hush," Mr. Burns hissed as he looked around in fear. "You keep your words to yerself." To Luke, he spoke low and quiet but with a deadly edge. "Mr. Morgan, there's people who went agin' Mr. Peterson and who no longer walk this earth. I don't aim to be one of 'em. I'm afeared for my job an' I'll keep my voice quiet."

"Then Trevor will control you."

"'Twill be better to be alive than dead," Mr. Burns said. "The men who go with Mr. Peterson fare better than the ones who stand up and let their pride stop them."

Nothing Luke said could change his mind. His hope of getting some type of help from the Irish workers went up in smoke.

I'm on my own.

Unsure what else to do, Luke walked away from the sad group. Luke found his own cabin still standing. He gathered blankets, a jug of water and the few food supplies he had on hand. He took them to the Burns family and gave them to Timmy's da.

"You don't need to tell anyone where this came from," Luke told the reluctant man, "and if you need more, feel free to visit my cabin."

He had no idea when—or if— he'd be back there again.

***

"Luke!"

Luke jumped at the sound of Davis's voice, terrified the man knew what he planned. He pocketed the small gun he'd made for Molly. At the cabin, he'd made sure to get the gun and plenty of ammunition.

I won't kill him unless I must.

"What are you doing?" Davis asked, coming from behind a railroad car.

"Thinking about some food," Luke answered, stalling for time. He didn't trust Davis enough to speak what was really on his mind. For all he knew, Davis too was involved in the selling of the women. "I've been trying to help some of the workers who lost everything in the fire."

Maybe Davis needed a reminder about what the town had endured that night.

"Well, think about eating some other time. And no need for you to worry about the workers, they'll be taken care of. I need you back at your workshop to finish those parts for the crates. We have to move faster than we planned. You'll have to work through the rest of the night."

It was the last thing on Luke's mind, but he quickly saw it might help somehow. "I'm almost done with them," he lied. In truth, Luke had finished the parts a day earlier, before he'd left to meet Red Cloud. Luke kept his voice calm and steady even though his heart jumped like grease in a hot skillet. "Would you like me to take them to the railroad car and rivet them into place when I finish? It wouldn't take me long."

"No," Davis shook his head, dashing Luke's hopes, "we can handle it. You've given us the pages of specifications and where everything goes. I've got other men to do the job. Just get the parts done on time and I'll send someone with a wagon to get them. In an hour or so. Until then, I have other business. This fire has derailed my plans."

"It wouldn't be any trouble."

They don't trust me.

There weren't many times in his life when Luke feared death was near. As he stood before Davis, Luke felt a dread he'd never known before. *They might kill me this time. To keep the secret.*

Never!

I must save myself so I can save the women.

The plan would have to be as intricate as any gun he'd ever crafted. And he didn't have much time to create it.

Chapter Twenty-Three

Where should I go, what should I do?

After he left Davis, Luke spent the rest of the worrisome night hiding out in an abandoned railroad car parked on the siding. He'd managed to snag a tattered blanket from a clothesline, intent on replacing it, and struggled to get a few hours' sleep.

Each time he dozed off, another thought tormented his mind. *Molly is stuck in that wagon with the other women*! Luke had no idea how or why Molly had approached the wagon. *Just like a woman.* He'd told her to wait for him to come back. Apparently, Molly had taken matters into her own hands. When he got back to where he'd left her safe and hidden, Molly was nowhere to be found. Afraid she'd been captured, he'd crept, heart thundering, toward the wagon. Close enough to hear Molly speaking to Priscilla and then Trevor. Now she was trapped too.

She knows I'm out here, somewhere. Will she be frightened I might get caught? Can she calm the other women? Or will one of them give me away, tell Trevor I'm out here waiting?

And what if Trevor insisted on dumping little Bonnie in the woods somewhere before morning? He could easily go back on his word to Julie.

Harry, I promise I will protect your family!

Luke's mind darted from one frantic possibility to another. He remembered Trevor's words to Molly spoken with a quiet hostility that chilled Luke's blood. *He truly is evil.*

Maybe it had been the way Luke had been brought up, but he'd always looked for the best in everyone. Even Trevor. He disliked the man, abhorred his cheating and lies. But until

Trevor spoke to Molly with such disgust Luke had felt Trevor might redeem himself if caught.

He only loved her because of her beauty and her purity. Probably didn't want to soil himself with a woman of another race. How he must despise himself for falling in love with Molly, a lowly Irish lass.

"I'm not getting any sleep tonight," Luke whispered in the dark, just to hear a human voice, even his own. He had never felt so alone.

Finally, he sat up. No use trying to sleep.

I need to talk to someone powerful enough to stop Trevor. Someone like Grenville Dodge. But how to get him to believe me?

Trevor had been hired by someone in the UPR – so he must have presented a good front. What if Dodge were in all this with him. But as Luke shivered through the night, he didn't believe so. From what he knew of the man, Dodge kept his actions honest. Unlike some of the other robber barons he'd read about, Dodge never seemed to rouse the newspapers' ire.

"General Grant is a good judge of character," Luke reminded himself, "He praised Dodge often enough. Surely, he would know if Dodge had a darker side."

Sometime before dawn, Luke decided his best plan would be to talk to Dodge. In person. Before the worker's had been killed by Red Cloud's men, Luke had thought of writing Dodge a letter to explain Trevor's shady schemes. While the meeting with Red Cloud, the fire, and then finding the women in the wagon had pushed the idea from his mind, Luke knew Dodge had to be told. The idea of informing Dodge was still sound.

It would either work or not. He had to team up with someone else who could stop this madness, and who better to protect the railroad's supplies than the man who'd created the railroad itself? And even if Dodge wouldn't help stop the trafficking, help save Molly and the other women, his help would enable Luke to do what was right. Like a well-balanced trigger mechanism, solving one problem would give him the power to stop the other.

Surely, Dodge was not someone who would condone a "hell on wheels" following the UP tracks? Hadn't it been Dodge who ordered General Casement to "clean up" the town of Julesburg? If not, Luke was determined to cross that bridge when he came to it. There had to be others who would stop this craziness.

Luke had done what Trevor wanted, made the fake parts to hide the crates of moonshine. If he were Trevor, he'd want to get rid of anyone who knew about his schemes. Like some of the Irish workers who'd been killed. Luke didn't know why. Mr. Burns would certainly not confide in him, but Luke assumed it was because they'd been asked to take part in one of the illegal activities.

Probably killed to keep them quiet. Just like Greg.

Luke had to wonder if the fire and Harry's death had been a part of that. The conversation he'd overheard in the woods seemed to hint at an accident, but Luke wondered. Greg's death had been deemed natural too.

I sure wish Greg were here now.

A rooster gave a croaky, sleepy alert. *Rockaroodleroo…*

Almost dawn.

Silently, Luke peered from the railroad car, careful to glance around. The streets of the town seemed empty. Near the Labor Camp, campfires still burned and there was a low murmur of the immigrants. He had a brief thought about who might be cooking breakfast with Molly in the prison wagon. Or even if there was breakfast to prepare with the mess tents in ruin. So much destruction!

He had no idea in mind except to find some type of proof he could show to Dodge. Then find a way to meet up with Dodge in person while keeping away from Davis and Trevor. Then save the women. He'd had more complicated task lists in the weaponsmiths' tent during the war, but not by much.

Sneaking silently through the darkened streets, Luke made his cautious way to Davis' office. His heart thumped almost out of his chest when a low growl came from behind.

Turning, he saw a mangy hound, sniffing around.

"Shush, boy," he spoke softly, "it's all right."

The dog came up to sniff Luke's boots and wag its tail at half-mast. "Sorry, fella, nothing to give you."

As if he suspected as much, the hound turned and snuffled down the dirty road.

Quietly, Luke eased into Davis cubbyhole of an office.

I'll take some of the requisition papers! That will prove the theft anyway.

The room was dark; the fingernail moon had moved behind a cloud. Dawn was just a faint pink tint in the eastern sky. Luke didn't dare light a lamp. He managed to strike a match and hold it over Davis's desk. The man was untidy and there were papers piled everywhere.

Luke took care to return everything to the same place each time he lifted a stack. No sense giving away that someone had been here. Although how Davis could find anything in this mess was a puzzle. He went through almost all the matches in his pocket. Finally, when he'd almost given up, Luke investigated a leather mail pouch Davis had hung on the door.

Paydirt!

There were two letters addressed to the UP office back East. Without a qualm, Luke ripped them open and found several of the illegal requisition papers. Including another for fifty more crates of moonshine and one for a dozen cases of expensive whiskey.

Luke slid quietly out of the office and by a roundabout route, made his way to the shed with his forge. To his utter horror, Timmy Burns and his gap-toothed friend were sitting on a wooden box, waiting.

"Hi there, Mr. Morgan," Timmy grinned. "We came early cause you promised Joe you'd make him another little gun. His got dropped an' a wagon done run over it. We was runnin' to get away from the fire."

"I'm sorry, boys." Luke's heart pounded, more afraid for the boys than for himself. "You'll have to leave. Someone is coming and you shouldn't be here."

I shouldn't be here.

Timmy's green eyes peered into the lightly gray shadows of dawn beyond the shed. "You in trouble, Mr. Morgan?"

"No, I..."

Yes! I'm in trouble! I don't want anyone to find me before I can get back to the wagon with Molly and the other women.

"Me an' Joe kin help," Timmy assured him.

"You can't," Luke started to say, his mind darting to a way to fix this, to keep the boys safe. If Davis came to pick up the metal and saw them...but what would he think...the boys had just come to wait for a toy. "Well, maybe you can. You know Mr. Davis Jones?"

Joe puckered his lips and made a sour face. "That ole crow. He's mean."

"Is he after you?" Timmy asked.

"In a way. Listen, boys, if I hide can you tell Mr. Jones you saw me earlier? Tell him I said I'm going around looking for Mr. Miles' wife, Julie. I can't find her anywhere. Can you tell him that?"

"Sure."

"I can't stop to make you another toy right now, but later I will. I must do something very important, and I don't want Mr. Jones to find me until I do. Do you understand? You mustn't give away my hiding place."

They nodded solemnly.

"He's going to be looking for those metal pieces," Luke pointed to the neat stack of parts he'd forged. "Tell him I said his parts are there."

Luke wormed his way between two piles of lumber and put a keep-quiet finger to his lips. Both boys gave him eager grins but thankfully turned their backs on his hiding spot. He prayed the boys wouldn't give him away. Settling behind the lumber, he kept a wary eye on the shed and waited.

Davis and a group of men came to pick up the metal pieces in a wagon.

“Where’s Morgan?” Davis shouted at the boys. He stomped into the shed, peered at the cold forge, and came close to the lumber. “Why isn’t he here?”

Peering around the wood, Luke watched Timmy shrug. “Gone.”

“Gone where?”

Timmy lifted his bandaged arm and shoved a lock of red hair off his forehead. “He’s lookin’ for Mr. Miles’ wife. She got lost.”

“In the fire,” Joe added solemnly. “When he finds her, he’s gonna make me a toy. He said you was to take that pile there.”

Joe pointed to the fabricated parts.

Davis snorted. He turned to several men in the wagon. “Go ahead and load the pieces,” he instructed. “Careful now, don’t bend any of those! We need to be able to rivet them in place once we get to the railroad car.”

After the men had gently placed the large metal plates and covers Luke had crafted in the wagon, Davis glared at the boys. “Tell Morgan I’ll be back to see him later. Do it, you hear, or I’ll whip your hides.”

Luke stayed hidden until the men had finished loading the wagon and rumbled off. Davis followed behind on his black and white horse.

He took time to ruffle Timmy’s red hair and chuck Joe under the chin. “Thanks, boys, you helped me a lot. Now, don’t tell him which way I’ve gone. When I come back, we’ll make those toys.”

If I come back.

Chapter Twenty-Four

"Halt right there!"

At first Luke thought the words had been directed toward his hiding place in the crook of a half-dead oak. His heart stiffened and his breath caught in his throat. A second later, he realized it was just Davis, hollering to stop the men with the fake UP parts as they pulled up alongside the tracks. A railroad car sat on the end of the track – attached to an engine. A head of steam blew upwards a gray plume of smoke signaling a departure.

"Are we planning to take the women on here too?" Davis leaned from his saddle to speak to a man standing near the car.

Trevor!

Luke curled his lips in disgust.

"No," Trevor answered. "That lot is going to Kildare's Saloon."

"But that's thirty-five miles away!" Davis protested. "There's no way we can get them there on time."

Trevor nodded curtly. "Exactly. But we can't take them on the railroad cars. Grenville Dodge will be in town. We can only sneak the moonshine past him this time. I'm going to take the women in a wagon and keep them hidden until Dodge is out of town."

"Sounds like a good idea," Davis agreed. "Why's Dodge going to be there? I thought he was coming here to inspect the progress of the tracks."

"Oh, some fire an' brimstone preacher's been hollerin' about damnation and ruination. He plans to stop and see if 'hell on wheels' is real or not. He's had that General Casement trying to clear out the towns. And if that happens, we lose a lot of money," Trevor sounded as annoyed as if he'd like to strangle the preacher. "We can get ten times the amount they charge in Omaha for whiskey and moonshine. I'm not about to lose that profit."

"Casement? He the one who walks around carryin' a bullwhip?" an Irish voice asked from the wagon.

Davis silenced him with a thunderous expression.

"You men," Trevor shouted at the workers who'd brought the parts in the wagon. "Get those pieces inside and fit together. The rest of the men are bringing out the moonshine." When the men had hurried to carry in the metal parts, Luke watched another wagon pull up with the crates of moonshine. His heart lurched to see several of the Irish workers, including Timmy's da, among them. Sounds came from inside the railroad car as the men placed Luke's well-designed hidey-holes into their slots.

No wonder Mr. Burns didn't want to go up against Trevor.

"Once we get the train with the moonshine on the way," Trevor told Davis as they watched the men loading the redesigned railroad car, "I'm going to take the women toward the town a different way. You'll oversee making sure the shipment gets unloaded. It's going to take more than a day to move these women in the wagon. We can't come in and announce our arrival."

"We should have had that Morgan create some kind of hidey-hole for the women too," Davis chuckled. "A lot easier than packing them overland."

Trevor nodded. "Maybe next time."

Over my dead body!

Luke eased back into the woods, searching for the prison wagon. It appeared to be still hidden in a patch of pines. He didn't want to get closer in case there were guards. *Are the women all right?*

Finally, his patience was rewarded. He saw Molly's face at the barred window. A second later, Julie peered out. *They must be terrified, unsure what's going to happen.*

Luke could only hope Molly still knew he was out here waiting.

What if I can sneak into the wagon too? If he could get inside, he'd be able to travel along with the women. Somehow, maybe there would come a time he could approach Dodge or another higher official.

I can't do anything on my own here.

Luke's shoulders slumped, hopelessness a weight on his chest.

A soft scurry behind Luke made him swivel around as he pulled out his Colt. He held it ready, hand easing the trigger into firing position when from behind a pine he saw Muchen. The man's face twisted in agony, and he held frightened hands up to implore Luke not to shoot.

"Muchen!" Luke whispered, "what are you doing out here?"

He pointed toward the wagon. "My wife... Liling. Taken."

Luke started to ease the gun back into the holster but instead kept it ready. "I'm not sure what we can do, but follow me. I'm going to try to get in the wagon and hide."

Muchen nodded.

Now it was more dangerous, but Luke was glad to have someone along. They walked carefully through the woods and were nearing the wagon when Luke heard a sound that stopped him cold.

Two guards were headed their way.

"Hey, you!" A lean man in rough clothes hollered, pulling a gun from a holster tied around his leg, "Stop there."

"What do you think you're doing? You don't belong out here," the other man shouted. He didn't wait for a response before he fired.

The bullet missed, slicing off a branch half an inch above Luke's head.

It was instinct, although Luke had no forethought about it. He drew the gun and shot back at the man who'd fired at him. A bullet whizzed through the air and hit the man a direct blow to the heart. He was dead before his body plunged to the ground, spurs jangling.

The second man, wide-eyed at Luke's prowess with a gun, pulled his own gun and aimed toward Luke's head. Again, instinct surged and Luke drilled the man with a second bullet. He too dropped to the ground. Dead.

"Oh, God," he mumbled, sickened at the two bodies bleeding in the grass. "I hate killing."

Muchen had never moved, but stood, eyes wide in wonder, hands tucked neatly inside the wide sleeves of his tunic.

"No choice," Muchen murmured. "Save."

Luke shook his head, the contents of his stomach heaving. He swallowed hard. A shout from somewhere put wings on his actions. He slammed the Colt into the holster and motioned to Muchen.

"We need to hide these bodies. Someone heard. We can't be caught."

Even if he didn't understand all the words, Muchen was quick to follow Luke's actions. Luke grabbed the worn leather boots of the first man and dragged him into a pile of brush. He tugged some branches and pine needles to cover him. Not much of a grave, but maybe hidden until they could get away. Muchen followed his actions with the second man, surprisingly spry for such a short man. No wonder. He pushed loaded wheelbarrows of rocks all day. He must be a Goliath in a David-sized package.

"We need to hide."

Muchen nodded.

Luke placed one foot carefully in front of the other, aware that even a snapped twig could give away their position. Whoever had heard the gunfire might capture them.

A couple of men hurried toward the edge of a clearing. Luke saw them just in time to motion Muchen to hide behind some rocks.

"I know I heard gunfire," a southern voice drawled. "Ambrose and Cleon were out this way."

"Well, I don't see anything." The second man said. "Ambrose! Cleon!" he hollered. "Don't hear anything either. Probably snuck off to have a drink. Or off huntin' rabbits. Heard Cleon say he was hankerin' for a good rabbit stew. Let's get back to those women. I sure don't wanna get caught when Trevor comes back."

Luke's foot slipped and a twig snapped. He caught his breath. From behind the other rock, Muchen's dark eyes closed in prayer.

“Wait, did you hear that?”

“Hear what?”

“Branch broke. Mighta been a fox, might not.”

“You didn’t hear squat. Let’s go.”

“What’s your hurry?” one of the men said, pulling a flask from out of a side pocket. “Let’s set down an’ have a couple’a drinks for the road. Them women ain’t goin’ nowhere.”

“Well,” the first man drawled, “reckon it’s gonna be awhile before Trevor gets the moonshine loaded an’ gets back here with the other wagon. More’n an hour or so he said.”

The men sat on a fallen log, content to enjoy their drink—and one of Trevor’s expensive cigars, by the pungent odor that tickled Luke’s nose. Maybe it would keep them occupied for a while.

After waiting until the men began to share stories, one in a drunken slur, Luke and Muchen moved forward. Slowly.

Luke had a simple plan, but it required patience.

Chapter Twenty-Five

"An' we need to get out." Molly repeated.

Something she'd been saying ever since last night when Trevor had locked her in the wagon.

Molly had stood patiently after Trevor left the wagon. Somewhere out in the woods, she knew Luke had to be hidden. It was unthinkable that he might have gotten caught. After Trevor left, that day wore on into another night. They were given food, a bucket of water to share, another bucket to be used to relieve themselves. The stench in the wagon had risen as each of them modestly took care of necessary business.

"Can't have you arriving in bad shape," a rotten toothed man in smelly blue denim pants and a rugged jacket laughed when he came to empty the necessary bucket.

As that long night wore on, Molly became less and less sure about rescue. Once Trevor had left and the guards settled around the campfire, Molly tried to get Julie alone. They sat on the rough floor of the wagon, almost overcome by the nasty smell of unwashed bodies and the baby's soiled diaper.

"I'm so frightened," Julie whispered, trying to shush Bonnie's whimpers. "They only gave us a little food yesterday too. I tried to feed Bonnie but she's not able to keep much down. I haven't been able to nurse her much."

As Molly sat beside her, Julie pulled down her dress and put Bonnie to her breast. The baby tried to suckle, and finally fell into whimpering, fitful sleep.

"Luke's out there somewhere. He knows we're here." Molly tried to reassure the woman.

"What good is that to us?" Priscilla asked, overhearing the conversation. "He's one of Trevor's men."

"You're wrong."

"I was in the saloon. I saw him planning something with Trevor. How do you know he's not in on stealing us? I saw him agree to something."

Molly shook her head, although a seed of doubt prickled in her heart.

Where are you, Luke?

"Listen," another woman said. Molly heard the hard-edged tone of her voice. It was the mean-faced girl with thick lips who worked as a waitress at the Stanley House. "You've heard about those towns springin' up as the tracks move ahead. There're men setting up saloons, gambling dens and brothels all along the line. We're just part of the merchandise. Might as well just not fight it. I've heard some of those fancy women make a right smart amount of money. Maybe better than I make in town."

"You be keepin' your ideas to yourself," Molly snapped. "I'm going to get out, an' not be some rich man's plaything!"

A couple of women laughed at her. It didn't stop Molly from examining every inch of the wagon, testing the bars at the windows, even tugging at the padlock on the front. "I be thinkin'," she whispered to Julie, "we might be able to open that lock with somethin' long and thin."

"Like what? None of us have anything."

Molly scowled, racking her brain for anything they could use as a tool, but she didn't even have something as simple as a hairpin. The evening wore on.

Where was Luke? Why hadn't he brought help?

Molly prayed that he hadn't been captured too.

After she thought the men around the campfire had dozed off, Molly slipped to the front of the wagon. She'd found a small twig close enough to a barred window to pull through. She tried to put it into the slot for the lock. Wiggled it around.

"What are you doing?" Priscilla hissed. "You'll get us all in more trouble! One of the girls tried to escape and lost her food the other day."

"Mind your own affairs!"

Priscilla grabbed her arm and jerked Molly away from the barred door. "Leave the lock alone! Help me, someone."

Two other women grabbed Molly's arms and jerked her away from the door. One of the guards, hearing the scuffle, came over with a rifle in the crook of his arm.

"What's going on in there? You women quiet down or I might just have to pull you out for some punishment." He laughed a crude laugh. "Get some sleep. We got a long road ahead of us in the morning."

"See?" Priscilla hissed.

Molly yanked herself away from the women and went to sit near the back of the dark wagon. Only Julie came to sit beside her.

"Sure an' they're fools, not wanting to get out. We could all rush that man when he opens the wagon."

"If that Priscilla and her folk don't rush us right back," Molly growled.

Molly sat and fumed most of the night. At times, she dozed off, then her head snapped up as she caught herself.

Where was Luke?

Julie sat beside her, rocking baby Bonnie in a vain attempt to quiet the fussy baby. Eventually, the baby's head slumped into Julie's chest, and she fell asleep. "Oh, Lord, if Luke is out there somewhere, I wish he'd come."

"We need somethin' long and thin to pry at the lock," Molly whispered as the first faint rays of dawn poked through the windows. "Do you have anythin'?"

Sadly, Julie shook her head.

Molly clenched her hands in prayer. Then, as she often did in times of trouble, she reached under the bodice of her dress for the locket with Liam's hair. Holding it tight, she felt the shape again. *Ma's brooch!*

Long ago, before Liam left for the war, Molly had wanted a lock of his hair in the worst way. She'd seen a fancy gold locket in a shop window, but it cost more coins than she'd earn in a month. When she told Liam, he'd offered to make her a locket. The only thing of value Molly had brought from Ireland was Ma's brooch. A lovely golden pin with a fancy design of lily of the valley etched on one side. Worth hardly anything in coins, but it meant the world to Molly.

To keep from harming Ma's brooch, Liam had used the front for the locket and put a lock of his hair where the brooch's pin would be. He'd fashioned a second oval shape and welded the pieces together. Then he'd put it on a small gold chain.

"I've got something," Molly pulled the chain from around her neck and opened the locket.

Just then, a faint sound of gunfire reached their ears.

“What’s that?” Julie whispered. Although some of the women had shifted position at the distant sound, most still slept.

Molly stood to peer through the barred windows and saw the other two guards stand up and head off into the shadowy woods.

“They’ve left,” she whispered in Julie’s ears only. “Let’s see if this will work.”

Although her heart squeezed at the destruction, Molly knew it was just a piece of crude jewelry. She dropped the brooch to the floor of the wagon and stomped down with her boot. The small piece of glass Liam had placed over his hair shattered. Molly reached down, retried the precious bit of Liam, and picked up the broken locket. Just as she’d remembered, a long, thin pin lay hidden on the back of the brooch.

“This might work.”

Molly took her time going to the door of the wagon to try the pin. She had to be quiet as some of the other women had gone back to sleep.

“Saints, help us,” she prayed as she pushed the pin into the big hole of the lock. By twisting and turning, she finally heard a small snap and the hasp of the lock loosened.

We’re free!

Molly carefully unhooked the padlock and drew it through the bars. Julie’s eyes widened and she stepped carefully over several sleeping women to join Molly at the door.

“Where did the men go?”

“I don’t know. We need to leave now.”

"What about the others?"

Molly wanted to just run and leave the other women to their fate. But her conscience wouldn't let her. She bent down and shook Priscilla's shoulder.

"Huh, what..."

"We unlocked the door an' we're leavin'. You come too."

Priscilla's watery blue eyes bugged out. A couple of the other women woke up, stared at the door but refused to run. "We'll just get caught. It will be worse for us."

A Chinese woman near the back of the wagon stared at the open door with wide, dark eyes. Her face wore a look of acceptance, and she lowered her glance when Molly motioned her to come. "Come."

The woman muttered in Chinese and shook her head.

In the end, Julie and Molly were the only two who eased out the open door.

"Close the door," Priscilla ordered, "so we don't get in trouble for your stupidity."

Molly had no doubt the other women would give them away if they could. *Sure an' they're afraid.*

Bonnie began to whimper, the sounds loud in the early dawn. "You run ahead somewhere. Find help if you can," Julie said. "I don't want you caught because of us."

"I'm not leavin' without you."

Julie argued another second but didn't appear to want to go alone either. The two set off into the deeper part of the woods.

Although they tried to step carefully over the twigs, Molly thought they sounded like a herd of cows. A sudden movement to the right caused her heart to lurch. A man's strong hand reached out and covered her mouth.

Caught!

Julie's small, startled grunt told Molly she'd been captured too.

Raking her nails along the tanned hand holding her tight, Molly fought against the man's strong hold around her waist. Twisting and struggling, she jerked and kicked out as far as she could. Her hands yanked at the hand forced over her mouth. Frantic to run from the hot breath against her ear. It took a few struggling minutes for the words whispered in her ear to make sense. "Molly, it's me, Luke, you're all right."

Luke.

He pulled his hand away from her mouth. At the moment Molly had no shame, she was so overjoyed to see him that she hugged him as tight as she dared. After a second of hesitation, Luke returned the hug but broke away suddenly. Despite the circumstances, Molly felt a swell of hope, almost as if Liam had come to her rescue as he'd always done. The thought crossed her mind that Liam would have liked Luke.

"How did you get away?"

Molly turned to see that Muchen had caught Julie, now he smiled and bowed at her.

His wife, Liling, was one of the captives. Too bad she didn't know he was waiting out here for her.

"Where are the others? Did they get away?"

"They were afraid they'd get caught."

Luke led them a short distance away while Molly explained their escape. He gave Julie a warm blanket to wrap around baby Bonnie, then shared a canteen of water. Molly had never tasted water so sweet and pure in her life.

“What are we going to do?”

Molly wanted to stay calm, but she couldn’t. Any second Trevor would discover that she and Julie had escaped. She’d known enough of Trevor’s anger to know he would explode.

Worse than any fuse hitting a charge of black powder.

Chapter Twenty-Six

"Did you overhear any plans?" Luke asked.

Molly nodded. "Sure an' they plan to take us to a house of ill repute about thirty-five miles down the railroad. Priscilla says it be a hell on wheels town. An' Trevor's being all set to make a profit on each of us."

It stood to reason Trevor would sell contraband to the make-shift towns. He'd probably been doing it all along, overcharging the UP's investors and the government for moonshine, whiskey, and other supplies, then reaping a profit from the saloonkeepers and gambling dens. Luke figured Trevor had found another way to line his pockets by selling women too – women no one would miss like the lowdown Irish, Chinese and saloon girls.

Lord, help us.

"An' sure an' we need to get away," Molly spoke up, "before Trevor comes back."

"We heard gunfire and the guards went away," Julie said around Bonnie's fretful cries. "He could find us at any time. We must get away. They wanted to leave Bonnie in the woods!"

Luke had no doubt time was of the essence, but he didn't know what to do or where to go. They had to find a safe place for the women and little Bonnie.

"I have a plan to get to Grenville Dodge. I don't think he would condone this behavior of Trevor and the others. But I'd need to get to the town and meet him there. Davis took the last of the fake UP parts I'd made..."

Realizing he hadn't had a chance to tell anyone else about the scheme, Luke took a few precious minutes now to tell the three how he'd hoped to find proof of Greg's murder and to stop the illegal business of Trevor. "It's wrong to help Trevor do anything, but I felt there was no choice. But now I've put myself and the rest of you in worse danger."

"An' tis right of you to do so." Molly put a timid hand on the sleeve of his jacket. "I've a mind Mr. Bennett didn't die without help."

Luke managed a quick smile and grasped her hand, glad of the understanding.

Muchen and Julie both nodded as if they understood his reasoning too.

"Davis was looking for me. I managed to elude him but I'm not sure for how long." Luke looked around at the others, their eyes not condemning but looking to him for guidance. "I still feel someone needs to inform Dodge. I'd planned to leave and get to the town before Trevor and his men—but now..."

The women were free.

"I want you to be safe. We had to kill two of the guards. The others were looking for them. At any time, they'll be back to the wagon to wait for Trevor."

"I go save wife," Muchen declared and stood as if he prepared to go to the wagon.

"Wait," Molly said and grabbed the red tunic sleeve. "Most of the women are afraid they'll be killed by the guards if they try to escape. If no one knows we've escaped, maybe we can ride along to the town. Then Luke can come behind an' meet up with Mr. Dodge. I think we need to get back in the wagon quick."

"No," Luke shook his head, "I can't let you do that. It's too dangerous."

"No, 'tis not. They don't plan us harm, they'll be wantin' to sell us in right shape," Molly argued. "If you follow behind an' get to talk to Mr. Dodge, you can save us. We'll be safe until then."

"No, I won't let you," Luke repeated. "You'll stay safe out here and we'll figure another way."

"I'm goin'," Molly insisted, fists on her hips and green eyes blazing. One of her red curls had escaped the braid and dangled down a dirty smudged cheek. "An' I'm goin' before anyone knows we got out."

"What would be the purpose?" Luke asked, hoping to make her see reason. "You're out and safe. Now we can rescue the others."

"They won't come—some of 'em think you're in cahoots with Trevor. Pricilla saw you in the saloon."

Luke sighed. He'd figured Priscilla was hanging around their table with her ears pointed a little like a bird dog. If others thought he was in cahoots with Trevor, would anyone listen to his story?

I might be going to jail too. I did craft fake UP parts.

"I can't let you."

Molly drew herself up. "You're not sayin' what I can and can't do. I've had enough orderin' around from Trevor. I'll be getting back in the wagon and waitin' for rescue when you get Mr. Dodge to listen."

"What if he won't? Or I can't speak to him?"

"Then you'll find a way. I won't be afeared now I know you haven't been captured."

Luke shook his head but after a few more minutes of arguing, he agreed. "I guess I let you get yourself into this before and get caught. You may be right." He thought of the two dead guards in the woods. Remembering the other two sharing a flask, he felt a sense of urgency. "If the guards are found dead, but the women are still locked in the wagon, they can't blame you. I don't like it but here..." He thrust the small gun he'd made for Molly into her hand. "Remember how to shoot it." He managed a lopsided grin. "Don't be shooting yourself in the foot now."

"Sure an' you're..." Molly gave him a cheeky grin of her own but pocketed the gun in her dress. "Julie, you stay an' I'll act like you're still there."

"No, I'm going too." Julie's eyes were filled with tears, but she stood tall and gave them all a fearful, watery smile. "Trevor knows me. He knows who I am, and he will look for me. If you're going back, so am I. I don't want to cause trouble for the others."

"But what about the babe?"

Julie gave Bonnie a tender look, wrapped the blanket around her and handed her to Luke. "Can you take her to my friend, Maimie? She's got a mite too and can feed her. She'll be safe."

"What will you tell Trevor?"

Julie lifted her dress, ripped off a stained petticoat and wadded it into a bundle. While it didn't look quite like a baby, it might pass to an unsuspecting eye. "He'll never know."

"I can't believe I'm letting you do this," Luke said, "but it seems the best way. I will see you when we get to the town."

***

Luke stepped closer and Molly watched his head bend toward hers—almost close enough to land a kiss on her lips. Although she'd had to fend off many such moments with Trevor, Molly found her body leaning forward, her own lips parting, ready and eager to touch his.

Sure an' why would you be so bold, me girl? What would Ma and Da think?

At the very last second, maybe because Muchen and Julie were near or Baby Bonnie squirmed in his arms, Luke stepped back.

Just one look at his sweet face, the tears glistening in his blue eyes, and Molly knew.

Sure an' I'm in love.

***

He'd managed to see Molly and Julie safely back into the prison wagon.

Safely! I can't believe I agreed to this plan.

Thankfully, Muchen had distracted the two drunken guards away while Luke watched to see the women enter the wagon and clasp the lock closed. Molly had said they would tell the other women they'd changed their minds, were too scared to escape. There would be no reason for the other women to tattle on them.

Ha! Molly afraid!

Luke grinned as he made his way back to the railroad camp, watchful as always for anyone like Davis or Bruce Scott. He knew for his plan to work he needed to stay clear of anyone who might turn him over to the villains. Including the Irish workers. *Who can I trust?*

The baby whimpered in his arms, and he held her tight against his chest.

So like my little Hannah.

It had been surprisingly easy to walk into camp. Many of the men had gotten up, despite the fire the day before, and gone calmly to work. Things might happen at night, but the men knew their paychecks required them to show up, on time, to drive spikes, roll iron and all of the various other jobs. Only some women and children sat around the campfires, the smoldering remains of the camp still sending out puffs of smoke from the night before.

He found Miriam, Julie's friend, who asked no questions but took baby Bonnie into her arms. Several small children crowded around her, their eyes large and faces gaunt. Soot marred their clothes, and one little girl had a huge red burn mark on one bare leg.

"I'm Luke Morgan, Julie sent me to ask you to keep Bonnie for a few days."

The woman nodded.

"Listen." Luke dug a handful of Liberty dimes and half-dollars from his pocket. "Have one of the children buy some milk and bread from the store. Food."

Although she shook her head, Miriam's eyes never looked up from her intense gaze at those coins. "Please." He lifted her hand and poured the coins into her palm. "Julie wants you to have it."

Once he'd made sure Bonnie was safe, Luke made his cautious way back to the forge. Although the day rang with the sound of mauls driving in the spikes and men's shouts, the area around his shed was strangely silent. Luke grabbed a saddlebag and filled it with a few tools he might need. He also put in another gun he'd kept hidden under his wooden toolbox.

He'd left Muchen in the woods to keep watch over the wagon. Luke had a fairly good idea where Trevor planned to take the women, but just in case the plans changed, Muchen would be able to point in the right direction.

The next order of business was finding a horse. It would take too long to walk to the town where Trevor planned to sell the women. Luke knew he could easily rent a horse at the Livery in Council Bluffs, but would he be allowed? Without knowing who all was on Trevor's payroll, he might be walking into a trap. As much as he disliked the idea, Luke knew he'd have to borrow a horse—preferably without the owner's knowledge.

Luke found a horse, neatly tied at the back of the Stanley House. Face twisting in distaste for the necessary evil, he slipped the saddled horse's reins loose and led him down the dusty street. If stopped, he planned to say the horse had gotten loose and he'd just caught him. However, luck was on his side, and he got to the edge of the camp, mounted, and was off without getting caught.

I've not only crafted fake UP parts, now I'm a horse thief.

"You know what happens to horse thieves in these parts?" He said to the patient, plodding horse. "They get hung."

It was a sobering thought.

Chapter Twenty-Seven

The town where the next hell on wheels was being set up was about thirty-five miles down the road. It would be a long, hard ride—more than a day's ride.

As he rode, Luke planned what he'd do. He must find a way to meet Dodge and inform him of Trevor's illegal business. Surely any man with a decent bone in his body would abhor the trafficking of innocent women. The problem was—how to approach Dodge? He might respect Trevor for the progress of the UP's forward march toward meeting up with the Central Pacific. In his supervisory position, it was Trevor who had pushed the men to enormous amounts of work in laying the tracks. Dodge might like Trevor and be unwilling to admit the man had done anything illegal.

Still, Luke felt some hope in the fact that Trevor and Davis planned to keep Mr. Dodge in the dark about their activities.

If they had wanted Dodge to know, if he agreed with them, then why have me fashion hiding places for the illegal moonshine? It stood to reason that Trevor didn't want Dodge to know what was going on or to stop him. Heartened by the realization, Luke kept the horse to a steady pace.

"I'll have to tread carefully," Luke said to the horse, realizing he didn't even know its name. The saddle had seen a lot of use, the leather worn and comfortable. The horse too had seen plenty of trails and had an even temperament.

Luke stopped as often as he dared to let the animal rest and graze. It would take Trevor longer to arrive in town with a wagon full of women. Maybe not even by the next morning. Luke thought of Molly, Julie, and Muchen—all counting on him to get the job done.

It was a long night. Careful to keep away from any main roads, Luke had to circumvent the easier path to follow a faint trail of a road. At least he could see the survey stakes that led across the prairie, and that helped keep him on track.

Dawn was cresting when Luke finally led the tired horse into the tent city. This early in the morning, the dirty canvas tents stood silent, gaudy words painted across the fronts and sides. GAMBLING. RED EYE SALOON. DANCING. As Luke rode past, the faint scent of cheap pomade and whiskey wafted from one tent flap. An air of hopelessness seemed to surround the tents. Luke saw only one person near the tents, an old, hunched man pulling limp towels from a makeshift clothesline.

A larger saloon, made of gray weathered boards, testified to someone's hope there would be a real town one day. Another wooden building sported a badly painted board announcing *Hotel.* Across the front of the building a rickety porch held several men, enjoying morning cigars and a general air of camaraderie.

Luke rode close enough to overhear one man, dressed in an Eastern suit of navy-blue broadcloth, say to another, "I'm excited to see those new cars for the *General Sherman.* Grenville says it will be one of the finest showpieces around. Maybe even the one we pull into the half-way point."

"If those mucky-mucks in Washington can decide where that will be," another joked.

"I've heard somewhere in Utah," a third man added, "if the UP and the CP can agree. Still a lot of track yet to be laid."

Luke smelled the appetizing aroma of crisp bacon and fresh-baked bread. His stomach seized as he realized he hadn't anything to eat except for a few berries he'd foraged on the road last night. Maybe, after he spoke to Dodge, he'd buy breakfast.

The men had obviously ridden in this far on the newly laid tracks. A fine railroad car, glistening in the rays of dawn, sat on a siding. Festive flags and bunting draped the engine, the flags snapping in a slight breeze. As Luke watched, a man opened the rear door on the festive railroad car and walked down the short steps.

Dodge!

Luke had seen images of the man in the newspapers. A tall, dark-haired man, his beard and mustache were neatly trimmed. Piercing dark eyes under bushy brows gazed around as he surveyed the town. He stopped to straighten a dark blue coat, freshly pressed. His long legs wore black trousers, tucked into well shined boots. An elegant wide-brimmed hat, as befitted a former Union General, topped the dark hair. A braid of gold banding glistened in the early rays of the sun.

Luke dismounted, tied the horse to a nearby hitching post and walked toward Dodge. The thought crossed his mind that he should have taken the time to rent a hotel room and freshen up. *I look like I've ridden a day and a night to get here.*

Usually fastidious about his appearance, Luke knew time was too crucial to be bothered with life's niceties right now. He stopped Dodge as the man strode toward the hotel.

"Mr. Dodge, my name is Luke Morgan. General Grant often spoke of you, sir."

"You knew Grant?" the man asked, giving Luke a curious glance. His lips twisted with barely concealed disgust, no doubt at the dust covered trousers and rumpled linen shirt Luke wore. Both were mussed and looked as if he'd rolled in twigs all night. *Probably I did. I had nowhere to catch a quick nap but the ground.*

"Yes, sir, I served with the Ordnance Department as a gunsmith. I've also done some blacksmithing in my time. Sir, it's imperative that I speak to you about a matter of grave importance."

Dodge gave him a slow smile. "Isn't that what you're doing?"

"It's about something that's going on and I need your help."

"Everything all right here, Mr. Dodge?" One of the men from the hotel's porch came up with a suspicious glance at Luke, or his unkempt appearance.

Luke ran a hand through his light hair, aware that it felt dusty and disheveled.

"I'm sorry, I know I look like I've been riding all night, which I have," Luke hastened to explain. "The situation seemed to call for expedience rather than decorum. I had no time to dress properly."

The other UP men gathered around. "What's going on here?"

Luke took a deep breath. "I know you're come to inspect the railroad cars here. Trevor Peterson told me that you would be arriving. Also, that you are concerned about another "hell on wheels" town going up. Well, I must tell you I know things you do not. When you begin your inspection of the *General Sherman's* baggage cars, you will find a cleverly made—if I do say so myself—hiding hole in the car. It was designed to disguise fifty crates of moonshine and I'm sure at various times whiskey to be sold in these towns. All at great profit to Mr. Peterson and his men. Profits garnered by cheating the UP investors and the government by requisitioning supplies at over-rated charges."

"What? That's impossible! I've just done a short walkthrough of the car," a stout, balding man fumed, "There was no such thing."

"I will be glad to show you. I'm not proud of the deception, and I will take any justice you deem necessary. But it seemed the only way to prove myself to the men responsible for the murder of my friend. I was concerned that if I did not allow myself to participate in their deception, I too, would be killed."

"Murder?" The voices began to murmur.

"Are you suggesting," Mr. Dodge's deep, cultured voice asked, "that Mr. Peterson is responsible for this deception? What proof do you have if this is true?"

Luke shifted the saddle bag off his shoulder, opened it and pulled out the requisition papers he'd taken from Davis' office. "Forgive my boldness, but I took the liberty of taking these papers from Mr. Davis Jones' office last night. These are only a few of the requisitions I've seen since I arrived in June. There have been others for more supplies, including tin and tools, that I was forced to sign."

The men gathered around Dodge as he read over the papers Luke handed him.

"This is ...impossible..." the stout man murmured as he glanced at the papers. "How could this happen? He's cheating the investors out of..."

A second man agreed, "We must get to the bottom of this at once. Young man, I want you to show us this hiding hole you created. Is it full of moonshine at this moment?"

Luke gave a wary nod. "I think so, although I can't be certain. I saw the train loaded yesterday morning. Whoever expected a shipment here had plenty of time to unload it."

He hadn't seen Davis around town, but then, he'd had almost a day to settle his illegal transaction and return to Iowa.

"It's no matter," Dodge decided. "If the hiding space exists it lends credibility to this man's statement. We must assume he's correct and get to the bottom of this."

"Absolutely."

"Assuredly," the men all agreed as they gathered around in a circle.

"There's something else you haven't heard yet," Luke continued. "Trevor is also trafficking in women. He's headed here now with a wagon load of captured women to sell to someone in town."

"Unthinkable!" Dodge roared. "Rest assured, Luke, that we will do everything we can to save these women. This will not continue. The UP will not be besmirched this way. What would President Johnson say?"

They began to discuss plans until one of the men seemed to notice Luke again. "Young man, perhaps you'd like to rest and have breakfast? We'll keep a look out for this wagon you say is arriving. I'll alert the federal marshals if necessary."

"Thank you." Luke turned to head toward the hotel and then stopped. "Please, whatever you do, don't mention my name to Trevor."

I'd like to live long enough to know Molly survived.

Chapter Twenty-Eight

Molly prayed through the rest of the morning. Sitting beside Julie, she'd known in her heart Luke would find help. But some moments she doubted it. What if Trevor or his men caught him? How would he get away?

Thankfully, she and Julie had gotten back into the wagon just moments before the two guards came stumbling back, half-gone on liquor. They'd fallen near the campfire and as far as Molly could see, snored in sleep. They hadn't said anything about finding the dead men, so that secret would keep awhile.

To keep the other women from getting suspicious about their return, Molly put on a great show of not being able to find Luke.

""Tis a traitor he is," she made sure to keep the right tremble in her voice, although it was hard with her heart goin' *pit pat* at the mere thought of the man. She remembered the night her foot got caught, Luke asking permission to touch her. Sure an' a gentleman he'd always be—not like Trevor.

Julie went along with the show. "It will be all right, Molly, like Vena says—some of those women make a lot of money. Once the men trust us not to run away, maybe we can save some. It's not going to be as easy for me with Bonnie." She made a show of patting the wadded petticoat cradled in her arms. "But I aim to make a living for us somehow."

Molly let out a fake sob, although it wasn't as hard as she thought.

If anything should happen to Luke!

“Men,” Priscilla sneered, “good for nothing. All they want is one thing an’ they’re willing to pay a hefty price for that. I don’t reckon I mind much.”

“I’m thankful we got Bonnie out of here,” Julie whispered as she cradled the fake bundle and patted the “baby’s” back. “Even if I don’t survive, my friend Maimie will raise Bonnie and give her a good home. Harry did a lot for her when her husband broke his ankle. One of the iron rails rolled off a cart and almost crushed his foot. Harry fought Trevor tooth and nail to get Everett a job he could do while his foot mended.”

“Tis Luke I’m hopin’ to save us before we have to worry about survivin’,” Molly whispered back.

Molly ached to tell Liling rescue was near, that Muchen was outside the wagon, but didn’t dare. Liling did not appear to understand much English. Her jabbering might alert the other women.

Sounds from outside the wagon came to the women’s attention. Molly stood up, shaking the pins and needles out of her feet. She peered through the barred window. A heavy wagon clattered through the woods, a team of horses grunting and snorting, their shod feet coming down hard enough to send up puffs of dust.

“What’s goin’ on?” Priscilla grumbled.

The dawn had broken, and birds chirped in the trees, setting up their glad morning song. How Molly wished she were back in the mess tent frying up skillets of eggs and bacon for the men. Instead, she stared at the man she despised, riding up on a black stallion.

“You men!” Trevor hollered to the two men who had driven up on the larger wagon, almost as big as a Conestoga. “I want you to get those women into the box. Make sure none of them get away and lock it tight."

One of the men jumped off the wagon seat and began to pull aside the canvas sides curved over the top of the newly arrived wagon.

Under the flapping canvas covering, Molly saw a large, wooden box without windows. A series of small holes were punched around for air – almost like a traveling box for animals. In fact, Molly had seen a circus train once with a lion in a box such as that.

"Are they putting us in there?" Elvira screeched. "I can't stand closed-in places! I'll die! It's like a coffin."

"You hush that kind of talk," Molly retorted.

When Elvira kept on sniveling, Molly grabbed her by both arms and gave her a sharp slap across the cheek. The startled girl gulped a sob and stared, eyes wide as an owl's.

"We need to do exactly what they tell us. We're all goin' to make it out safe and sound."

"How do you know?" Priscilla sneered in her nasty voice, tugging at the soiled yellow silk dress. "Did your beau tell you that? Trevor's friend?"

"He's not in it with Trevor," Molly repeated, tired of explaining Luke. An imp in her mind taunted, *but he helped Trevor make the fake UP parts. Sure an' he's guilty of helping hide the whiskey an' such. Maybe he is not the man I think he is.*

He helped us back in here. Maybe 'twas a trick to sell us off. Maybe I just imagined he wanted to kiss me.

"You there!" The man she knew as Jeffers pointed a rifle at Molly. "You first. There's not enough room to stand, so you'll have to crawl inside."

Molly's heart quailed as she got out of the prison wagon and followed the man's orders. Trevor, sitting in the saddle, did not so much as glance at her. The wooden box did feel like a coffin, an overheated, crowded coffin after all the women had crawled inside. There was room to sit, but not to stand upright. Once they nailed the end shut it was dark with just those small air holes letting in light.

By listening closely, Molly heard the canvas cover being dropped to hide the box. A man climbed back into the wagon seat and snapped the whip. The brave horses struggled to pull the wagon. The wheels rolled a bare inch before it stopped.

"We're gonna need more horses," the driver shouted to someone, "this load's too heavy."

Another wait, some of the women whimpering and crying over the soft, sing-song voice of Liling murmuring her native language. Molly clenched her arms over her chest and tried to still the wild beating of her heart. She reached instinctively for the locket, then remembered it wasn't around her neck. In the pocket of her dress, along with Luke's gun, she touched Ma's brooch and Liam's lock of hair.

The little gun with the cool, smooth mother-of-pearl grip made her smile and quieted her fears. *Luke does care. He is the man I think he is.*

Someone brought another team, hitched them to the two other horses. Slowly, bumping over the uneven ground, the wagon wheels began to move forward. The day wore on and on and on...

Inside the box, the summer heat built up. Molly's red curls lay damp and sweaty along her scalp and neck. The green calico felt as heavy as a quilt. The other women complained and fussed, snapped at one another. It was hours until the women were allowed out, carefully guarded, to take care of necessary business in the woods. One of the men sent around a canteen of tepid water.

Trevor let them stand by the campfire and eat a gruel one of the men cooked in a pot. The taste was vile, but Molly ate it down while keeping close to Julie and "baby" Bonnie. So far, Trevor had made no more comments about the baby.

"Now, listen, all of you," Trevor put on his ingratiating smile. "As you can see, we're taking a little trip. We should make it there by tomorrow morning. I've arranged for some blankets to make the ride a little more comfortable. You'll get those after we stop for the evening. We'll stop once more for supper and then tomorrow, you'll be in your new lives."

Elvira screamed and began to run. It did her little good. One of the men who'd driven the wagon, a hefty, dirty man in ragged overalls and filthy red union suit, ran after her. He grabbed a long swatch of her auburn hair, yanked hard until she fell, and dragged her across the ground.

The others could only stand and watch. Molly clenched her fists in fury. One hand curled around the gun in her pocket. She wasn't sure she could shoot—even if she pointed in the right direction—but she wanted to kill the lout in the worst way.

"Let that be a lesson to you." Trevor's dark eyes stared hard at each of them. "No one tries to escape. Now, back in the box! All of you!"

With Trevor's loathing eyes glaring at her, Molly marched over and helped the sniveling Elvira to her feet.

Crouched back in the wagon, Molly clasped the gun and prayed as she never had before.

Chapter Twenty-Nine

Stomach comfortably full of crispy bacon, eggs and sourdough biscuits, Luke sat near the back of the saloon, waiting for Trevor to arrive.

Soon, there would be justice for Greg. Luke knew his murder might never be proven in a court of law, but having Trevor pay for his crimes would be justice enough.

As planned, Luke would stay hidden until it was necessary to show his face.

Grenville Dodge and the men from the UP had come up with a plan. When Trevor arrived, they would ask him to take them around and show him the newly redesigned *General Sherman* cars.

"If you are correct about these women being driven into town," Dodge had said when they discussed the plan, "then we will have guards waiting at every road to watch when they arrive. I have left orders the women are to be released and kept safe as soon as possible."

"What do you want me to do?"

Dodge gave him a quiet look of scrutiny. "I realize you want to be where things are happening, but I must ask you to be patient. Do you see that man behind the bar?"

At Luke's nod, Dodge continued, "My men are convinced Mr. Rose is buying the illegal alcohol from Trevor. He sells it to the workers for a hefty increase in price. I'd like you to stay and keep watch. Don't let him escape. My men are going to confront Trevor after we find the hidden spots you showed us on the railroad car."

Luke fidgeted, shifting his feet, and moving a white mug of coffee around and around on the table. *What's happening? Has Trevor arrived yet? Are the women safe? Is Molly?*

Despite the seriousness of the occasion, he couldn't help feeling a gladness and lightness in his heart. It was the first time since his family's death that he felt a chance of life being good again.

Do I dare hope Molly can care for me?

Throughout the next hour, he kept a cautious eye on Mr. Rose. The man stood behind the bar, all jolly good humor to a couple of UP officials who were sipping whiskey slower than any man alive.

A shout from outside the saloon drew Luke upright in his chair.

"Stop that man!"

"Halt!"

A gun retort shattered the stillness of the morning, coming close enough to rattle the stained glass of the saloon's front window. Somewhere, a woman screamed.

Luke jumped up, the chair crashing to the floor behind him. Running outside, he darted into a scene of chaos. There were men everywhere, Irish workers, UP officials, a man wearing a six-pointed star and a wide brimmed hat, and a scattering of women.

The first woman he saw was Priscilla from the Commodore, eyes wild and holding up the tattered shreds of the yellow silk dress, a few feathers floating from the collar as she ran. A woman from town ran out to her, gathered the frightened girl in her arms, and led her into a tent.

Molly. Where was Molly?

Luke ran down the unpaved street, stomping through puddles left from overnight rain. His eyes roved from side to side—watching the chaos as someone caught the men responsible for loading the crates of whiskey. Timmy's Da gave Luke a reproachful glance as a UP man put a pair of handcuffs on him. Dragged him to a waiting wagon with other handcuffed men.

From far down the street, Luke saw a crowd of women running toward the town, the UP officials or anyone who might help them. At first glance they were just a mass of calico, gingham and swatches of hair blowing in the wind, their faces a blur. Then he saw Molly.

Her bright red curls, disheveled but still bouncing across the shoulders of a green calico, brought a smile of relief to his lips. "Molly!"

Molly looked up, eyes locked on him, and ran straight toward him.

Luke held out his arms, anticipating the joy of Molly rushing into them. Instead, she stopped just out of reach, panting and gasping for breath. "He's got away," she struggled to speak, "an' worse an' that, he told one of the men to get to the telegraph operator." Her words came out in a rush through a flood of tears. "He's ordered that Scott to have his evil friends burn Council Bluffs an' the rest of the camp to the ground. He wants everythin' gone so there's nothing to prove his devilry."

The news stunned him.

This is all my fault. I should have told Dodge right away Trevor might retaliate against the people left at the camp.

Luke's conscience chastised him; how was he supposed to know? No time for recriminations. He had to save all those innocent people somehow.

One of the UP officials came out of the saloon with Mr. Rose, ranting and cursing, "I've done nothing wrong! Nothing! How was I to know Peterson hadn't bought that all proper?"

"Where did Trevor go?" Luke questioned Molly. Maybe there was still time to save the town.

Molly shook her curls, tears still streaming down her face, "Run like the low livered cuss he is," she gulped out, "him an' that Davis. Left us women to those men drivin' the wagon. Someone stopped them on the road and let us out."

Just then Julie ran up, "Oh, Molly, you're all right. Everyone went rushing away willy-nilly and I couldn't keep up. I dropped Baby Bonnie–" Her eyes were wild and half crazed; a dazed laugh escaped her lips. "Nut Bonnie's safe isn't she, it was just a bundle of petticoats...oh, Molly, I'm so afraid!"

"Julie!" Luke grabbed her arms and shook until the woman looked at him with some sense in her eyes. "It's going to be all right. We need to get all the rest of the women and put you somewhere safe. If nothing else, you're a witness to what Trevor tried to do."

"An' how do you plan to keep us safe?" Molly asked,

"I don't know yet; I need to find Mr. Dodge."

***

The UP had sent men on Grenville Dodge's orders. Even his most trusted official, Casement, had hurried to the scene of the labor camp hoping to save the town from complete destruction. The trouble was, most of the help was coming from towns further down the railroad tracks.

It was too little, too late. Trevor and Davis had a head start. They'd been able to commandeer the railroad car that had brought the stash of illegal moonshine. Before anyone could stop them, the engineer blew a hearty *whoo whoo* as the steam built up and they went clattering down the tracks.

Luke, Molly, and Julie boarded another railroad car with Grenville Dodge and hurried back to the camp. It took less time than riding horses as Luke had the day before, but still several hours passed before they arrived. Hours behind Trevor and his men.

"Sure wish this train could travel faster than forty miles an hour," Luke lamented to no one in particular. He sat on the plush seat of Grenville Dodge's private car and pressed his booted feet to the floor, urging the train onward. Smoke and cinders blew into the open windows and Luke's eyes watered. Beside him, Molly clutched her hands in her lap and gnawed at her lip.

What will we find?

The UP had sent reinforcements on the train and they arrived in time to prevent some damage. Still, Trevor had made sure to cause as much grief as possible.

As before, tents smoldered, a couple of the wooden buildings burnt down to ash. To Luke's grief, more of the Irish lay dead in the streets, covered with sooty blankets. Women knelt and wept beside the bodies, little children standing around with wide, shocked eyes. Some of the Chinese, fearful of being killed, refused to help even lift buckets of water to squelch the flames. They stood helplessly by as more of the tent city burnt, most of their meager possessions going up in smoke. People wandered around helplessly, eyes glazed. There seemed no hope anywhere.

"I should have been here," Luke said in anguish as he stared at the destruction, "I should have prevented this somehow."

"Sure an' how would you have done that?" Molly questioned in a reasonable voice while tears coursed down her soot-smudged cheeks. "You did the right best you could."

"It wasn't enough."

Again, Luke felt as if he'd fallen into a deep pit of remorse. He hadn't saved the town. He'd let them down. Just as he had his family during the war. Just like Greg and Harry.

I've failed everyone. Again.

Chapter Thirty

A day later, Luke did his best to calm the community. Although Molly and Mr. Dodge both assured him it wasn't his fault, Luke felt the weight of responsibility anyway.

I should have done something.

Grenville Dodge had to return East. "I will send help to rebuild the camp and town," he promised. "I'll send reinforcements and more workers to continue laying tracks. As sad as all this has been, we must keep to the schedule to meet the Central Pacific tracks. The government and investors are expecting us to. We've had hardships before with the Indians and disease. We must press on to finish building the railroad. This project is bigger than all of us, all the heartache. The best tribute we can make to the men who died is to complete the transcontinental. And we will see that Mr. Peterson and his men are brought to justice."

The only person the UP officials had been able to capture in Council Bluffs was Mayor Willoughby. Trevor, Davis, and Bruce Scott had conveniently vanished, after torching Davis's office and burning all Trevor's files. The telegraph office had also gone up in flames, destroying any written proof of their deceptions.

"People are angry," Dodge told Luke. "Rightly so. I have no one else to put in charge. Mr. Casement is needed further down the line to help oversee the building of a trestle. Please, do your best to settle the people here."

A command Luke did not take lightly. Although he knew with his mind he could not have prevented Trevor's actions, in his heart Luke felt compelled to action.

Many of the Irish had broken into fights between themselves, angered over Luke's role in having Mr. Burns and his men arrested.

Hoping to speak to the people and calm them, Luke had gone to the camp. He soon found himself surrounded by men, women and children, faces glaring with anger or distrust. Tight-lipped and scornful, the people gathered around ready to spew their wrath.

"Please, listen to me," Luke held up his hands when the crowd edged closer, "it was not my intention for any of the workers to be arrested yesterday."

"An' why should we be believing you?" one woman spoke up.

"Yeah," Iris, one of the girls from the cooking tent, stepped forward boldly, "Why should we trust you? Maybe you're in it for your own self—skimmin' profits off the railroad too. We done heard how you crafted them parts to hide the whiskey."

Molly stepped up, "Yer daft, girl. He had ta do that or be killed."

Until then, Luke hadn't realized Molly had followed him.

"An' what about Burns?" A ragged voice shouted above the crowd. "An' the others just doin' their job?"

"I'm sorry," Luke told the man named O'Reilly, "Mr. Burns knew what he was doing when he broke the law. I've spoken to Mr. Dodge about the extenuating circumstances and how he feared for his life. I've been assured that there will be a reduced sentence for all the Irish who were forced to commit wrongdoing. Perhaps no sentence at all. It will just take time to sort things out."

"An' what about you, Mr. Morgan," O'Reilly raged back. "You crafted those illegal parts for Trevor Peterson? What makes your hands lily white?"

"It's true," Luke agreed, "but I did it for a reason."

He had spoken at length to Grenville Dodge and been assured he would not face charges.

"If you had not drawn our attention to the deception," Dodge said, "we would never have been able to stop it."

"An' maybe my Tim had his reasons too." Mrs. Burns raised a fist toward Luke. "Like keepin' the wolf from the door and his family safe. Why's he bein' blamed an' you aren't?"

"Believe me, Mrs. Burns..." In the crowd Luke noticed young Timmy, a sorrowful expression on his freckled face.

I've disappointed him.

"I will do everything I can to see that your husband and the others are given leniency. They were threatened and coerced by Trevor. They didn't do wrong willingly."

He would too. He had already spoken to Grenville Dodge about the Irish workers forced to haul the crates and the women. While some had been willing parties, others had done evil out of necessity or fear. It would take time to sort out who was guilty and who was not.

"Words, just useless words," Mrs. Burns spit out.

"He bribed some of you." Luke ignored the faces condemning him and forged ahead. "But you can break free of Trevor's evil net. If we join together, we can stop him and Davis. We can attain justice for the men who died. We can begin again, together. Your husbands and brothers will be freed."

"Is true," Muchen's voice raised behind Luke. Gladdened by the reunion with his wife, Muchen had followed Luke the past day like a loyal guardian. He had taken Luke to explain to the Chinese workers who feared the loss of their jobs and scant pay. Muchen and Liling had explained how Luke had saved the women. "You listen," he told the Irish surrounding them now. "He tell truth. We fight. We join," he clenched both hands together as if showing a stronghold. "We take back camp. We work."

It might have been Muchen's fervent words or the fact that little Timmy Burns burst out of the crowd, threw his arms around Luke's waist, and cried out, "I believe Mr. Morgan! He's a good man!"

Luke could never decide which action turned the tide in the crowd's opinion. As he patted Timmy on the back, he heard murmurs and grumbling. O'Reilly gave a snort of disgust and stomped away. A couple of other spike drivers followed. But in the end, most of the crowd began to agree with Luke. He heard several encouraging remarks, had men come up to slap his back. Muchen and the Chinese surrounded him with support. Before long, Luke knew with a deep assurance that whatever it took, the people were behind him. They would find Trevor and the others and take back their town.

Whatever it took.

***

Later that evening, Luke walked over to the forge. He stood under the open air shed, so weary he could barely stand. The night had cooled and as dusk came on birds began a sleepy twittering. Somewhere in the distance a lone coyote howled. The sound pierced him to the core.

What a lonesome sound. He felt the same lonesomeness as an intense pain, a longing for something. No, *someone.*

Looking out as the sky darkened and tiny pin pricks of stars began to glisten, he thought of Harry and Greg with a sadness difficult to express. Greg's murder would probably always be considered a natural death. There was no proof unless someone confessed. Luke didn't see that happening.

"So, an' there you are," a soothing voice spoke from behind him, "I've been looking for you."

"Molly," Luke turned to see her standing there in the half light of the new moon. She'd cleaned herself up since he'd last seen her. There had been little time for any of them to change clothes, wash, or even comb their hair in the mad rush to return to Council Bluffs. Then the scramble to help those who'd been injured during the second fire.

It had only been later, after facing the crowd, that Luke had managed to get a bath and clean clothes. Molly must have done the same. She wore a pale blue dress with a lacy collar and cuffs, and her lustrous red curls hung past her shoulders. In the moonlight, her green eyes shone above a quivery smile.

Luke's heart clenched in sudden realization. *Her, I long for her.*

I love her. When it had happened, he didn't know. Molly had crept into his heart and taken it over.

"Molly." Even to himself his voice sounded husky. The right words would not seem to come.

Maybe it didn't matter. Molly crossed the grassy floor and came to stand before him. "Yes?"

"Molly," he whispered again and drew her into his arms. She fit snugly against his chest, just as he knew she would. Holding her tighter, he dropped his chin to the top of her soft hair, inhaling the scent of rosewater and fresh soap. "You're beautiful, did you know that?"

"Sure an' you be tauntin' me with such words," she whispered against his chest but didn't pull away.

He tipped her head back and stared down into those emerald green eyes. Even in the moonlight they glistened like jewels. "I love you, Molly McGregor."

The words came with a hitch as she asked, "Do ya' now, a lowly Irish like me?"

"I love everything about you." His throat felt choked with an emotion so powerful he knew there was only one thing to do. One way to express the deep longing he suddenly felt wash over him.

Luke bent toward her face, his cheek against the soft smoothness of her own, and pressed his lips to hers. Hungrily, as if he'd been starved for years, he kissed her over and over. Her lips, her cheek, her hair, her neck...the sweet soft curve of her throat...

He felt her yield and meld into his embrace.

Somewhere in a split second, while he tried to get his breath, Molly muttered, "Sure an' what would me Da be sayin' about this? An' us not proper wed?"

A chuckle escaped his throat. For the first time in far too long, Luke felt whole again.

Chapter Thirty-One

Luke couldn't stop a grin from crossing his face as he walked toward the Stanley House the next morning. *Molly loves me.* Last night, when he'd reluctantly let Molly leave to join Julie in a room at the Stanley House, Luke couldn't stop grinning. *Molly loves me!* Although he thought nothing could change the cloud of happiness surrounding him, a voice called out, "Luke! Hey, Luke."

He turned and waited as Charlie, one of the men who had worked for Harry, ran down the dusty street. Behind him were several of the other Irish workers, carrying picks and rifles.

"Listen, a couple of the men know where Mr. Peterson an' the others are hiding. A lot of 'em are wantin' to go capture the cowardly scum an' make them pay for what they done to Harry and the others." Charlie shouted. His bushy red eyebrows squirmed across his forehead—rising and falling as the words rushed out with determination. Harry had often called Charlie a "hothead just spoilin' fer a fight." Seeing the man's green eyes fill with righteous anger, Luke could agree.

"Are you certain?" Luke asked.

Charlie nodded, bitterness flavoring his words. "The curs—Trevor Peterson, Davis an' that Bruce Scott are hiding out in a farmhouse about three miles away from here. I've got a crew of workers all set to go capture 'em, if you're in Luke. We'll string 'em up from the nearest tree."

One of the workers waved a pick with a menacing gesture. "I say let's go get 'em now."

Turning at a slight gasp, Luke noticed Molly watching from the hotel porch. She pulled a white lace shawl across her shoulders and looked down at him.

Oh, Molly.

He remembered the sweet taste of her lips on his, her soft curving body and the gentle touch of her fingers on his cheek.

"Molly?" he questioned. It was up to him to end this here and now—to help the men capture the others. But, if Molly feared too much, he would not. She had suffered too much from Trevor already. He would not force her to wait behind while he headed off to confront the man.

"Sure an' you best be the one leadin' the others, Luke," she said in a quiet, reassuring voice. Only he could tell by the pinched look around her green eyes it was an effort for her to encourage him. "They need ta be caught. But not for stringin' up." This time she gave the men a stern look. "They need ta be caught for the law to deal. An' pay for what they done."

"Luke?" Charlie questioned. "Are ya' comin'?"

Luke turned to see others in the community coming toward the Irish workers. Some led horses, a few had piled into the wagon—holding pitchforks, shovels, and more rifles. Muchen led many of the Chinese workers on foot.

They were all set to take down the criminals, to wrest their town back from the wrongdoing they'd suffered and to complete the monumental task of building the transcontinental.

"Yes, I'm going too." There was no other choice.

***

Three miles out of town, they came upon an abandoned farmhouse, the shingles weathered and falling off. Luke remembered Harry telling him the family had sold it to the UP for a good price. The newly laid tracks gleamed in the morning sun where they crossed what had been a hundred-acre corn field.

I hope they received a fair price, Luke thought irreverently, as he rode toward the house in one of the wagons.

Before the crowd could move toward the shabby porch, a shot rang out from a broken window.

"Get back!" Davis shouted. "Get back or we shoot!"

"Everyone back," Luke hollered, although most everyone had turned to retreat. A few men hunkered down behind the wagon. Others crouched near the barn or in a small orchard. There were small sounds—men coughing, branches snapping, some whispers and one lone rooster heralding the dawn. Other than that, each sit stood silently by.

Watching.

Waiting.

"What should we do, Luke?" one of Charlie's men asked. "I can't say I want a bullet through the heart."

Luke studied the situation. Although he had brought more men with him, Trevor and his men had a stronger position. Inside the house, they could see everyone, pinpoint any target. They could aim and hit any man they chose.

We don't know where they are. We're at a disadvantage.

"Let me think a minute," Luke answered, studying the house from all angles. Anyone who tried to rush toward the house might be shot. Even sending someone around back to sneak in might result in more deaths. There was only one thing to do. Get Trevor and his men out of the house.

How?

Muchen moved slowly up to Luke's side. "We shoot?"

"No," Luke shook his head, "maybe it's time to think like Trevor and give him a taste of his own medicine. When he wanted to destroy the camp, he used fire." Luke looked around at Charlie and a group of the Irish workers. "Maybe it's time we start a fire of our own and force them to surrender."

A grin widened Muchen's face and his eyes crinkled into long lines. "I go," he said. Before Luke could agree to this plan, the man had slipped away.

Not long after, Luke heard the distinct crackle of fire eating into wood. However Muchen had managed, he'd set fire to the back of the farmhouse. A dark plume of smoke rose from the kitchen area. In minutes, the old wood had caught, sending forth black rolling smoke and eating away at the shingles.

"Come out, all of you!" Luke shouted.

A gunshot rang out the window, along with a gray cloud of eye-watering smoke.

"Let 'em burn," Charlie's eyes narrowed, face furious. "Like Harry."

Davis came running out the front door first, coughing into a sooty handkerchief, waving his gun in the air. "I surrender. I surrender! Don't shoot."

Two men ran forward, caught him, and tied ropes around his arms and feet. Bound, they hauled him into one of the wagons. The next man through the door was Scott. Coughing worse than Davis, he ran outside and fell, face forward in the dirt, gasping for air. A couple of the Chinese workers caught him and bound him too. He was also led to the waiting wagon.

"Come out, Trevor!" Luke called, "you don't want to burn to death. The men have agreed you'll face the law. We won't harm you."

A shot rang out as Trevor aimed through the window, flames crackling as more glass broke.

Luke had brought his gun along, but he saw no need to use it. "Trevor, you don't have a chance! Come out, give up."

It's up to you. Surely, even Trevor Peterson would choose survival rather than burning alive.

The crackling of the flames ate away at the front porch roof. An orange red glow shone through the windows. The heat grew so intense, the crowd of men moved back, leading the horses away. One horse, fearful of the flames, reared and snorted.

Luke feared Trevor would rather die from the smoke or flames than face the law—or anyone he'd harmed—but as the roof caved in, Trevor stumbled out the door. Face blackened by the smoke, coughing and choking, gun held in a limp hand. Charlie started forward but Luke held him back.

"Let me talk to him."

Luke marched forward where Trevor leaned over, hands on his knees. As Luke came up, Trevor glared at him with disdain, straightened and went to the horse trough to splash tepid water over his soot covered face. The water left wide ribbons of white and dirty skin.

"Now you see what Harry saw in his last moments," Luke said, "right before he died in a fire your men set."

"You can't prove anything," Trevor spat out. "Harry was a fool."

"Was Greg too? Or did he refuse to go along with your illegal activities once too often?"

Trevor wore a supercilious grin. Even with dirt smudging his face, his blue suit rumpled and sporting several burned spots, he stood tall and acted as if he owned the world. "You have no idea who you're dealing with, Morgan. I have friends in very high places. You may have talked Dodge into stopping us for now, but there's a fortune to be made while we build this railroad, and you haven't stopped us yet. So don't think you are a hero. You are a nothing."

"I don't have to think anything," Luke said quietly, knowing in his heart he was no hero – only a man trying to do the right thing in a bad situation. If there were any heroes, they were men like Greg and Harry who had died to see the transcontinental railroad reach from coast to coast.

"C'mon Peterson." A man Luke hadn't noticed came boldly forward. He wore a six-pointed star and a wide-brimmed Sheriff's hat. "I've been sent to take you into custody for…"

Luke stood and watched as the man led Trevor to join Davis and Scott on the wagon. It was over.

Chapter Thirty-Two

The new telegraph operator in town, sent to replace Bruce Scott, passed along the glad tidings the next day.

All arrested near Kildare Saloon. Dodge says all in custody. More to follow.

The news spread throughout the camp. Even though most of the men went willingly to work that morning, plans were made for an evening of celebration. Firecrackers, a dance, a community dinner—there had never been such a jollification. The Irish and Chinese workers scurried about after the day's work, setting up plank tables and clearing off a tamped down square in the middle of the town for dancing. Many of the women cooked all day over campfires to produce a meal with all the food sent by a grateful Grenville Dodge on one of the railroad cars.

"This town is busting with good news," Luke said as he buttoned the cuffs of his best linen shirt. He turned to Julie, who had offered to help iron his best clothes and who knew what he planned for the evening. A plan she'd approved of with a wise knowing smile.

"I've good news too," Julie said as she helped brush the dark broadcloth suit Luke planned to wear to the dance. "All the girls sold before ana' one found out about the trafficking business were found. I heard tell from Charlie and Priscilla. All the brothel owners been arrested and the women released."

"That's good news." Luke agreed. He thought of Aura Lee and wished her well. It gave him hope things could turn around for the labor camp now that Trevor and his comrades had been captured.

"The UP has found new men who will run the project now. So, we don't have to put up with the likes of Trevor Peterson or Davis again. Mr. Judah is sending a new surveying team and Mr. Dodge will make sure the engineers are respectable men." Luke took his suit coat from Julie and shrugged into it. Stood for a final inspection as Julie studied his appearance.

"Sure an' you're a handsome lad," Julie said. "People are asking you to take over for Mayor Willoughby. To be the new mayor of Council Bluffs. I've heard plenty talk of it."

Luke flushed, pleased but knowing he'd refuse. "That's a tribute, but I've decided after the UP meets up with the CP, I'm going back to New York. Back to my ranch. Home."

Right before she left his cabin, Julie gave him a cheeky grin, "An' I expect you won't be goin' alone, Luke Morgan."

Again, his face flamed. *Is it so obvious?*

At the dance, he couldn't wait to get Molly off to the side and ask her the important questTime seemed to drag as slow as the starting *chuga chuga* of a train building up steam. After a few fast square dances, the makeshift orchestra of two fiddles and a mouth harp began to play a slow, sweet version of "I've Left the Snow-Clad Hills." Luke could remember hearing the Swedish nightingale, Jenny Lind, sing it in Manhattan. The sad, plaintive tune about a young girl pining for love made Luke's heart beat harder.

"Molly, I know this will seem quite sudden. I'm not even sure how much longer we will be out here working on the railroad." Luke swallowed hard. He'd gotten word the day before that the UP and CP were set to meet tracks at a place called Promontory Point, Utah in May '69. "I've set to stay on until the tracks meet, but then I'm hoping...praying... Molly McGregor, will you marry me?"

Those green eyes shone with a joy he felt matched his own. His heart lurched in his chest and he couldn't stop a wide grin. "Sure an'..." Her voice choked. "Sure an' you're a bold one, Luke Morgan. Go to kissin' a girl so she can't get her breath then ask a question such as that! I'd be wantin' a wedding by a priest. Ma and Da would want to make certain it was proper."

"I've already telegraphed Omaha and spoken to a priest who's willing to marry us day after tomorrow. The tracks will be arriving in Nebraska about noon."

"An' what would we do then?"

"We'll need to stay on until the transcontinental is finished, but then we can leave. I'd hoped you would accompany me back to my ranch in New York. It's a fine place, Molly. Good land. I've a workshop there handed down from father to son. Maybe one day, we will have a son to pass it down too."

Molly flushed. "An' you're movin' a bit too hurried for me. I'll need a spot of time to answer."

"Do you think you could say yes?" Luke couldn't keep the eager tone out of his voice as he bent closer to her. "Before we get to Omaha tomorrow?"

"I be thinkin' I'd like to say yes if..."

"Anything. I would give you the world if I could."

Ducking her head, then glancing up at her with a timid smile, Molly asked, "Would you be sayin' we can bring Julie an' wee Bonnie along too? They have nowhere to go an'..."

Luke pulled her into his arms and smothered her with kisses. When she could struggle out of his embrace, she asked in a breathless voice. "Am I thinkin' then you answer yes?"

"Yes, yes, my sweet Molly. Anything you ask of me. Anything and always."

It would only be fitting to help Harry's family get a new start. Luke thought his heart might burst from the front of his linen shirt. He could see baby Bonnie growing strong and healthy. Maybe one day playing with their own children—his and Molly's. Julie could be a big help to Molly as they worked to rebuild the ranch. And Molly...his sweet, green-eyed Molly, by his side giving him hope for the future. Somehow, in his heart, he knew Betty would approve.

***

My wedding day.

Molly stared at the sun beaming into the hotel room through a lacy curtain. She turned as Julie lifted the shimmering armful of lace and satin gown and dropped it over her red curls. "You'll look so lovely," Julie murmured as she tugged the shoulders into place and helped Molly pull her arms through the sleeves. A mirror over a well-dusted bureau gave Molly a glimpse of herself. It was enough to take her breath away.

Surely, only a princess would wear a dress such as this. The floor length gown of satin had an overlay of fine handspun lace sewn with a pattern of roses. Luke had seen it in a dressmaker's window and insisted on buying it for her when they'd arrived in Omaha that morning. Although Molly had thought nothing of being married in her best dress, mended only slightly, the gown had taken her breath away.

"I never believed this would happen. That I'd be wed proper in a church an' my heart so overflowin' with love."

Julie smiled, although tears filled her eyes. "Oh, Molly, you're beautiful. You and Luke will be so happy with one another. And I thank you for wanting to take me with you when you return to New York."

Turning to face her friend, tears shimmered in Molly's eyes. "Oh, Julie, 'tis I who should be thankin' you for comin' along. I'd be afeared to start a new life, even with Luke, an' leave you here. I always asked Ma, why can't I have a sister? An' Ma would say, 'when God's ready, he'll find a way to give you one.' Today, it's like God answered me prayers an' I couldn't have a finer sister."

"I feel the same way," Julie whispered, wiping away her own tears.

They looked at one another and then hugged, until Julie fretted that they were mussing the dress.

It was soon time to head for the small, whitewashed chapel. As she neared the doors, knowing her future awaited on the other side, Molly felt a flutter of fear. Almost, she turned and ran. *Sure an' what right do I have for happiness? Liam, dead and buried. Ma and Da so far away.*

"I'm afeared," she whispered to Julie, holding tight to her arm.

"So was I," Julie spoke calmly back, "it will all disappear as soon as you see Luke. I promise."

The doors opened. Charlie, Muchen, so many of the other workers she'd known crammed into the six or seven wooden pews lining each side of the aisle. The Burns family—Timmy grinning a gap-toothed grin. Iris, Clover and even Priscilla in a new calico dress, lower cut than proper, but still decent. Tears filled Molly's eyes at the thought of them all caring enough to come see her wed.

Molly looked down the worn, red-carpet runner and lifted her eyes to the priest standing at the altar. A short man with bushy dark hair and wearing a dark green vestment, he gave her an encouraging smile. Standing to his right...

Julie had spoken true. As soon as Molly's eyes looked on Luke's she saw nothing else. In her fine, new dress, the satin shimmering and rustling, Charlie led her down the aisle. He'd offered to stand in for Da—so far away in Ireland.

"Slow down there, Molly me girl," Charlie whispered as the tiny organ began to play a wedding march. "Some might be thinkin' you can't wait to get wed to Luke."

"Sure an' they'd be right." Molly grinned and clutched the tiny bouquet of daisies Luke had picked for her.

A beam of sunlight chose that second to pierce through the stained-glass window. It made a path up the carpet toward Luke and the priest. With a heart overflowing with happiness, Molly followed it toward a life she had never imagined.

Chapter Thirty-Three

Morgan Ranch

New York

May 1870

"Kathleen, now there's a good Irish name," Molly Morgan said as she put a glass of lemonade down on the table. "Could be Katie for short," she mused, swiping a tired hand across her forehead.

"I like either one," Julie Miles said as she got up to peer over the veranda railing. Four-year-old Bonnie was content on the spring grass, chucking happily as a brown and white puppy with long ears licked her chin. "Bonnie, you stay where I can see you now."

"'Es, Mama," the little girl lisped.

"Are you certain you're in the family way again?" Julie asked after a sip of lemonade. "Little Greg's not even a year old yet."

"Well, not for certain sure," Molly mused as she glanced down the pea gravel drive at her tall, sturdy husband.

Molly grinned to herself, remembering the feel of Luke's arms around her and the sweet way he loved her. *Sure an' Ma was right such moments were left to the bonds of marriage. T'wouldn't have been proper to let Trevor take what rightly belonged to Luke.*

A contented gurgle drew Molly's attention down to a patchwork quilt on the veranda where ten-month-old Greg Bennett Morgan, named after Luke's friend on the UP, played with some wooden toys. He babbled in baby talk and gave Molly a drooly smile. "I'm not sure for certain, but I'm thinkin' possible."

Julie gave Molly a wise smile. "I think a woman knows. I did with Bonnie, before Harry and I even thought such a gift was possible." She blushed, "We'd only been wed about three weeks, but I knew."

Molly glanced at her friend. It had been hard for Julie to leave Harry's grave in Iowa, although the fire had left little to bury. Luke had insisted on a fine marker for Harry, even mentioning how he died saving Timmy Burns. "I'm glad you came to New York with us, Julie. You've been a help all these past months gettin' Luke's house cleaned and fixed. I'd not have done it alone with Greg gettin' teeth and squalling half the night like a banshee."

"I'm glad too," Julie answered, "and maybe God had a hand in it. If I hadn't come here, I'd never have met Jedediah."

"As me Ma used to say, 'Molly me girl, when we think there's no hope, God's already pullin' back the curtains on a new day'."

"That's a lovely thought," Julie smiled, going to check on Bonnie again. "It's true enough for me. I thought I'd never love another man after Harry died. But coming here, meeting Jedediah, God knew all along our hearts needed one another."

Jedediah Montgomery, Luke's long-time neighbor, had been a widower for over ten years. Although slightly older than Julie, he'd take a shine to the sweet-tempered, lively woman and the spritely Bonnie. His sons were all grown and away. Although no one had set a date yet, Molly had her suspicions it wouldn't be long. An' sure and God knew having Julie nearby would help once she had this next sweet babe.

"What if the baby is a boy? What would you name him?" Julie turned back to the conversation.

"Tis a girl," Molly spoke assuredly and placed a hand over the middle of her blue sprigged dress. "An' the more I think, the more I'd like to name her after Ma."

It had been so long since Molly had a letter from the folks in the old country. Neither Ma or Da had ever learned to write. After Liam died at Chancellorsville, she had sent a small letter to the parish priest to give them. He had replied that they wanted Molly to come home if possible. By then, Molly had thought she would wed Trevor and stay. She'd never imagined her life would turn to the UP and that she'd end up with the true love of her life, Luke.

Some afternoons, Molly walked to the small family graveyard and had a quiet conversation with Betty, Luke's first wife. She wanted Betty to know she loved him and cared for him just as she would have done.

"What was your Ma's name?"

"Mary. Mary Margaret McGregor."

"That's lovely too."

Someday, maybe they could take little Greg and Mary Margaret to Ireland. If a railroad could span from one end of the country to the other, anything was possible.

"Well now, Bonnie," they heard Luke speak up from the edge of the yard, "I have to fix this gate. It's gone all rusty and I don't want any little girls to get hurt on it."

"Now where has that child got to now," Julie jumped up in exasperation. No doubt little Bonnie had turned into a handful once those small feet had learned to walk.

Molly laughed. "Followin' after me husband, she is."

Molly and Julie walked to the end of the pea gravel drive; baby Greg perched on Molly's hip.

"Are you bothering Luke?" Julie questioned her daughter with a stern expression in her eyes.

Bonnie looked up, eyes open and honest—the spitting image of Harry's green, twinkling eyes. "No, mama, honest. Mr. Luke said I could help."

"Now Bonnie..."

"It's all right," Luke smiled up at them. "I told her she could hold the screws and hand them to me."

Bonnie kept up a cheerful chatter, full of questions. Luke patiently answered every one until Julie decided he'd had enough.

"Come now, it's time to fix supper. You can help me."

"But I want to help Mr. Luke make the gate."

"Bonnie Miles!" Julie kept her voice stern. "Do you want to stay here when Mr. Montgomery takes us buggy riding after church tomorrow?"

"No, no, I'll help," the little girl handed Luke the leather pouch of screws and hurried to obey her mother. It seemed a grief to Molly that Bonnie would never remember Harry. But Mr. Montgomery cherished the little girl and would raise her up right.

"Let me take Greg and put him down for a nap," Julie held out her arms for the baby. "Give you and Luke a chance to talk a spell." She gave Molly a wink behind Luke's back.

Molly gave her friend a grateful smile, her arms aching from Greg's study but heavy body. He'd drooled all over her dress shoulder, cutting teeth.

Once Julie and the children had walked toward the house, Molly went behind Luke and spanned his waist with her arms. She pressed her face against his warm, somewhat sweaty shirt, and hugged.

"And to what do I owe this attention?" He asked as he pulled her around, a teasing glint in those blue eyes. "Not that I mind, of course."

"Luke me dear, would you want to welcome another wee one soon?"

His eyes opened wider, and his delighted smile went from one sunburned cheek to another. "You think so?"

"I'm thinkin' maybe along about next February."

"Nothing would make me happier, and you know it." He leaned over and kissed her deeply.

It was hard to pull away, but Molly knew he wanted to finish the task before dusk settled over the valley.

"Do you want to help me? I've just got to put this gate back on the hinges. You can help me hold it upright."

Molly had heard the story about Betty's fancy gate. The one Luke had forged right before the war. The war between the states. How long ago it seemed. The same time that she'd been a scared young girl, coming over on the long sea voyage with Liam from Ireland. Fearful and excited at the same time. America was a grand country, full of promise and enough food to fill their bellies at last.

"What are you thinking?" Luke asked as he screwed in a bolt and stood back to look over his work.

"Oh, just about me past, leavin' Ireland an' comin' to Iowa."

"If you hadn't come, we wouldn't have met."

"Sure an' I know," Molly spoke slowly, having a hard time putting her thoughts into words.

Father O'Bannon had written back when Molly told the home folks about her marriage—right and proper—to Luke. They sent congratulations and prayers for the future. In later letters, she'd shared the news about baby Greg. Only Ma returned word to say Da had gone to join Liam in an everlasting reward.

"What are you thinking?" Luke asked. He tested Betty's gate to see it had the proper swing and began to gather up his tools.

"Do ya' ever think of the others, Luke?" Molly asked, a worried tremor in her voice. "An' wish they still be here with you. Instead..."

"Instead?"

"Instead of me?"

"Molly Morgan." Luke put down his toolbox and came to draw her into his arms. "I think of Betty and the children all the time. But I don't wish they were here instead of you. God has reasons for things, my sweet Molly, and I don't pretend to understand any of the whys. A long time ago, I stopped trying to make sense of the world. I only know there are times when God puts us in a certain place at a certain time. He puts people into our path for reasons only He can know. Just like He put you into my life."

As he squeezed her tight and planted a kiss on her neck, Molly relaxed into his sturdy embrace.

"Sure an' why would He be doing that?"

"To love." Luke looked into her eyes with so much devotion Molly's doubts were put to rest.

Epilogue

Morgan Ranch

New York

May 1873

Three years later

"Why, Poppa, why?"

Luke Morgan grinned down at his four-year-old son, Greg. Early that morning, when Luke headed to his smithy, Greg tagged along like a persistent shadow. The little boy had stood respectfully at a distance while Luke fired up the forge and selected metal bars to begin a new project. The distance didn't stop Greg's chattering. It reminded Luke of times past.

"Why, Poppa?"

So like Billy used to be. Although the memories pained him at times, Luke tried to remember his first family and cherish all the sweet moments they'd shared.

"Poppa?" Greg interrupted his thoughts, "are you making shoes for horses today?"

"Sure an' there you are, Greg," Molly interrupted as she came to the door of the workshop, one hand holding tight to three-year-old Mary Margaret. The little girl with a head of bouncy red curls like her mother danced in her fancy new slippers. A new lavender dress, Mary Margaret's favorite color, swirled around her tiny body.

"See, Poppa?" She lifted one foot and then the other. "New shoe. Me go visit Miz Julie."

Luke grinned at his daughter and up at his wife. "You're going to see Julie? Would you like me to hitch up the buggy?"

"No," Molly answered, "Mr. Stevens has got us ready to leave. I come to see if Greg wants to come too an' play with Bonnie. She sent word special she's got a new pony."

"Aw, she's just an' old girl," Greg sneered, although he and Harry's Bonnie had been fast friends since they were both small. "I want to help Poppa."

"It's all right," Luke agreed, grinning at the pleased expression on Greg's chubby face. "I could use a helper today."

Molly glared at her son, shook her head, and turned to lead Mary Margaret away. "We'll be home near lunch," Molly said, "An' Mrs. Clemmons says she's fixin' one of her Irish stews. Just for you."

"My favorite."

Luke watched Molly and a prancy Mary Margaret walk toward the buggy. One of their servants, Mr. Stevens, a freed Black they had met while working on the Transcontinental Railroad, helped Molly into the shiny black buggy. A fine Arabian stallion, dark brown hair gleaming in the sun, pulled them down the pea gravel drive. Molly gave a little wave, cut short by having to grab their daughter to keep her pitching sideways during a vigorous wave of her own.

"What are we makin', Poppa?" Greg asked. "Shoes for horses?"

"Not today. I'm just trying to repair this trigger guard on Mr. Montgomery's old rifle. He's had it for a long time and hopes I can fix it."

"Can you?"

Luke grinned as Greg pulled up a stool and perched beside the workbench. "Sure enough."

Luke picked up a small pair of pliers and an even smaller screw. Repairing guns came easily to him. Even easier than the fine ironwork gate he'd created for Betty that long-ago week after Fort Sumter had been fired upon. How long ago it seemed. How far life had taken him since those long-ago days.

As he mended the gun, stopping now and then to answer his small son's questions, Luke couldn't help but think about how far the years had brought him. From shattering loss to monumental achievement. He and Molly had ridden back east after the trains had met. They spoke of someday traveling coast to coast, passing towns they'd known well—Council Bluffs, Omaha, all those towns crisscrossed by shining steel tracks.

"I like Mr. Montgomery," Greg said. "An' Miz Montgomery too. She makes good oatmeal cookies."

Luke grinned. How Harry would be glad to know Julie and Bonnie had found a home with his neighbor.

"We'll always remember Harry," Julie had told Luke and Molly on her wedding day, tears glistening in her eyes, "but Jedediah has given us a future. He will take care of us just as Harry would have done. Harry will forever be in our hearts and I will make sure Bonnie never forgets him."

While Luke had offered to have a marker put up for Harry near their new home, Julie refused. "There was nothing to bury," she spoke sadly but practically, "an' we never did have a grave for him in Iowa. I think Harry would not mind. He never was one for fancy markers an' such."

"Greg? Did I ever tell you who you're named for? A friend of mine I met while working on the transcontinental railroad."

Greg's face grew pensive. He struggled to form the question, "What's a ...tran...con...what's that, Poppa?"

"The transcontinental railroad. It was a railroad that went from the east coast to the west coast. Men built it over several years. My friend, Greg Bennett, was a locomotive engineer. He could drive the railroad cars."

This was something interesting to Greg's little mind. He loved to visit the railroad depot in town and watch the arrival or departure of the trains. "Then that's what I will do when I get big like you, Poppa. I will drive the trains too."

Luke laughed. "Maybe you will. You can be anything you've a mind to, son."

Little Greg hopped off his stool and went to pick up a couple of sticks. Soon, he was engrossed in a game of soldier or cowboy, using the sticks as pretend weapons. Luke watched him with a thankful smile.

I am so blessed.

Luke knew it was only God's providence that had kept him safe all those years during the war and after. He was the most appreciated gunsmith in the area, doing work for the Ordinance Department and the cadets at West Point. He was also one of the wealthiest people in the area, able to give Molly, the children, and his servants anything they could need or want. Although Molly would be just as glad to wear cotton and homespun, Luke delighted in giving her dresses crafted by a private seamstress. Gowns rich in satin, lace, and velvets.

He and Molly made it a practice not to spoil their children, or even little Bonnie, their goddaughter, but they would never have a true want in their lives. If Greg wanted to learn to become a locomotive engineer, Luke could and would pay for the finest training to make it so. He hoped to some day turn his workshop over to Greg, if the boy showed an aptitude for gunsmithing or even blacksmithing.

Luke stopped as another memory came to his mind. A conversation he'd had with his first son, Billy. Betty had made a remark about Luke being a blacksmith for the day.

Billy wore a perplexed look and ignored his mother. "But Poppa, you're a gunsmith. How can you be a blacksmith too?"

Betty laughed, the sound like a delicate wind chime. "Your Poppa is a master of many trades, Billy. He made all the handles and candlesticks in the house. As well as most of the gate latches and things we use every day."

"He did?"

Embarrassed at the worship on Billy's face; Luke was nevertheless pleased. "Gunsmithing and blacksmithing are both kinds of smithing, Billy. Even though a person makes different things with each trade, they have a lot of skills and tools in common. Both use a forge and an anvil. And both smithy's use forging, hammering, and filing. It just makes a difference what you happen to make – a gun or iron work."

Betty gave him a worshipful smile not unlike Billy's. "We've worked hard to get to this position of wealth. I don't think it's unseemly to show the rest of the world. You can be an example to others, Luke."

Is that what I am? An example to others?

Luke thought of the years he'd spent working with the railroad. Of trying to bring Trevor and the others to justice. He'd just been doing what he felt was right. Had God been there all the time, putting him in the right place at the right time?

As he looked at his tow-headed son, so much like the older brother he'd never known, Luke couldn't help a warmth swell his heart. He thanked God for a second chance at love with Molly and for two more children to love. Evil had taken away Billy and Hannah, but God had given him Greg and Mary Margaret.

There could never be enough words to shout his heartfelt gratitude.

I'm truly blessed—my cup runneth over in abundance.

THE END

Also by Zachary McCrae

Thank you for reading "**Forging Destiny** "!

If you liked this book, you can also check out **my full Amazon Book Catalogue at:** https://go.zacharymccrae.com/bc-authorpage

Thank you!

Made in the USA
Columbia, SC
26 April 2024

34945270R00134